Buffalo Township

Buffalo Township

Lauran Paine

THORNDIKE
CHIVERS

This Large Print edition is published by Thorndike Press®, Waterville, Maine USA and by BBC Audiobooks, Ltd, Bath, England.

Published in 2005 in the U.S. by arrangement with Golden West Literary Agency.

Published in 2005 in the U.K. by arrangement with Golden West Literary Agency.

U.S. Hardcover 0-7862-7807-2 (Western)
U.K. Hardcover 1-4056-3474-X (Chivers Large Print)
U.K. Softcover 1-4056-3475-8 (Camden Large Print)

The text of this Large Print edition is unabridged.
Other aspects of the book may vary from the original edition.

Set in 16 pt. Plantin by Liana M. Walker.

Printed in the United States on permanent paper.

British Library Cataloguing-in-Publication Data available

Library of Congress Cataloging-in-Publication Data

Paine, Lauran.
    Buffalo Township / by Lauran Paine.
       p. cm. — (Thorndike Press large print western)
    ISBN 0-7862-7807-2 (lg. print : hc : alk. paper)
       1. Large type books. 2. Western stories. gsafd I. Title.
    II. Thorndike Press large print Western series.
    PS3566.A34B85 2005
    813'.54—dc22   2005010031

Buffalo Township

CHAPTER 1

Women Named Elisabeth

His name was Douglas McLeod but they called him Lodestone and when he died, eventually, they put it upon his headboard as 'Ludston'.

'D. Ludston, born Scotland, died Montana Territory', and because they had no clear idea when 'D. Ludston' had been born and were not sufficiently interested to make an effort to find out, they did not put down a year. They knew when he died but they did not put that upon the headboard either because it would have implied that he had been born in a particular year and someone probably would have made themselves obnoxious about it.

D. Ludston had been an impressive man in only one way. Otherwise, he was nondescript, lacked a very well-developed sense of humour, said very little, worked day and night and remained pretty much to himself. But he could handle whisky better than most other miners in the gold camps, and although he was slightly less than average in height, he was an uncommonly accurate shot with either a rifle or a pistol, so he had the respect of his acquaintances if he never won either their affection or their complete acceptance.

His one remarkable attribute was that the summer he took in the half-breed woman who had fled the camp of a *voyageur* named Devaux, was also the summer he found his Smiling Woman mine.

Before D. Ludston died he owned two-thirds of the bank-stock in Buffalo, Montana, half the business buildings on Front Street, and the sprawling, big thriving cattle ranch he had rarely left the last years of his life. He and his half-breed woman lived there together as compatible as peas in a pod. She was almost as taciturn as he was, but she had a better sense of humour and was a counterbalance to his parsimony. She would stand up to him, too. There were oldtimers around the Territory who could cite instances they had witnessed when she had put both hands upon her hips, had fixed him with her tawny stare, and had without saying a word, worn him down.

She had been a handsome woman, a shade taller than Douglas McLeod, with golden skin, jet-black hair and gold-flecked dark eyes. They had lived as man and wife for thirty-seven years and the year following his departure, she simply sat down and waited a short while, and also died.

By then her daughter Elisabeth was two-thirds grown and the little, private cemetery upon its tree-shaded knoll behind the ranch-house, held the graves of her two sons within the scroll-work iron fencing. Both the boys had died very young.

Now there were more graves beneath the recurring springtime hair-fine delicate grass. D. Ludston was out there and so was Smiling Woman, whom he had always called Elisabeth because that had been his mother's name.

There were also the graves of several rangemen who had died from one cause or another upon the ranch. Two had been ambushed by Crows, killed, and had had their hair lifted. They were among the first residents of the private ranch cemetery. After that, with the passing of the hostiles and the taming of the land, rangeriders who had been killed upon the ranch or had died from one of the epidemics which regularly passed through, were put down in an orderly manner as though ranch policy had arrived at a conclusion that there would be more and more graves over the years and therefore it might as well become Ludston practice to conserve space and arrange the graves in neat rows the way it was done in the towns.

By the time there were eleven graves in the ranch's private cemetery Smiling Woman's daughter, Elisabeth, was also out there, and her consort, a well-bred, well-educated good-for-nothing named Albert Bedford, was also out there, and Elisabeth's daughter, also called Elisabeth, owned all the Ludston holdings and operated the vast Ludston ranch.

Her name was Elisabeth Ludston Bedford. She was a little above average height for a woman, had dark grey eyes which seemed to pale out, and also to darken, with her passing moods, reflecting a strong-willed nature, and it was said of Elisabeth L. Bedford that when she cracked a whip every grown man in the town of Buffalo and half the grown men in the Buffalo territory cow country jumped a foot.

She was twenty-six years of age, had indifferently turned aside the offers of friendship, and other things, of every man she had thus far encountered, stood erectly handsome, and muscular, more man, some of the town-women said, than woman.

She had somewhere along the line picked up someone's blunt forthrightness. It could have come from her grandfather, or it might also have come down to her from Smiling Woman; it was occasionally recalled that when Smiling Woman was angry and had something to say, she said it, but wherever Elisabeth L. Bedford got the attribute — or fault — from her grandfather, her grandmother or some other progenitor perhaps even farther back, power and wealth lent this facet of her nature a strong kind of support, as when she was informed by her rangeboss, Art Campbell, there were free-graze cattle on Ludston range.

'Get them off,' she had said quietly, looking Campbell squarely in the eye, 'any way that you have to.'

Art Campbell took all five of the Ludston Ranch riders to the grazer's camp that evening, burnt everything which responded to a torch, shot two men, neither seriously, stampeded all the free-graze saddlestock, and stood the headman of those troublesome, raffish people beneath a huge and ancient oak tree and gave him sixty seconds to defy the Ludston holdings and get lynched on the spot, or to agree to be off Ludston range by sundown of the following day.

In Buffalo, people who ordinarily sympathized with cow-interests who routed free-graze people, listened to what Campbell had done at Elisabeth L. Bedford's command, and said absolutely nothing at all, but the next time Marshal Everett Monday saw Campbell in town he bluntly gave it as his opinion that sooner or later Elisabeth L was going to lock horns with a winner instead of a loser.

Lanky, mildly arrogant Art Campbell had quietly agreed with that. 'Yes, Sir. And we got eleven graves at the ranch with room for one more.'

Jack Lewis of the *Buffalo Bank & Trust Company*, a Ludston adjunct discreetly informed a number of close friends that when wealth was aligned with strength it amounted to power, which was exactly what Elisabeth L had.

Homer Bevans of the *Big Valley Liverybarn Inc.* was somewhat like Marshal Monday in his opinion, except that Homer lacked Everett Monday's patience, and when he said Elisabeth L would run into the wrong person one of these days he was hoping very hard that it would happen soon, no later he told Ev Monday, than by the end of this riding season.

It was easier to discuss probabilities than to either visualize them eventually occurring or recognize them when they arrived.

Nor was there likely to be any haste about a forthcoming confrontation with Elisabeth Ludston Bedford. Art Campbell was a bad man to cross with fists or weapons, and he did not hire men he would ever have to make excuses for. Wherever the SM brand was seen people knew *her*, the kind of men she had riding for her, and the kind of wealth and power which she possessed. No one ever went out of his way to seek a confrontation.

Elisabeth, on the other hand, was not generally difficult. She knew her rights, affected no compromise with respect to them, did whatever she had to do to ensure that she and her rights were never challenged. But otherwise she ran her ranch, supervised her investments in town, discreetly avoided social engagements, and evidently enjoyed being slightly aloof and quite solitary.

No man including her rangeboss, her

riders, her tenants in town nor any other individual of the opposite sex called her Elisabeth to her face. But everyone, of both sexes, called her 'Elisabeth L' behind her back. They threw in the 'L' to differentiate between the Elisabeths of the tribe. Someone had started that when she had been a child and people still did it although her mother was no longer living, although, in fact, there was only one Elisabeth Ludston Bedford.

She knew it; knew exactly what they called her and what they said about her, and none of it bothered her one bit. She was, as Beulah Lewis, the banker's wife often said, as near to being a self-sufficient individual as there was in all of Big Valley, Montana, and perhaps anywhere else.

She rode like a Sioux and rumour had it that she could curse like a freighter. She bossed her own gathers and ran her own marking-grounds, when she was on the ranch, otherwise Art Campbell did those things.

People had once linked those two names but one night in Buffalo at the saloon Art Campbell had flatly said he would not ever marry a female like Elisabeth L if he lived to be a hundred and fifty. She was, he told the entire roomful of men, everything he did not cherish in womenfolk and that by gawd was a damned fact!

After that, with no other name to link hers with, people dropped all speculation about Elisabeth L's prospects, and concentrated instead upon the other varied and colourful facets of her character, but, as Everett Monday said, giving his moustache a twist, it was a blasted shame that a woman built like that, as strong and supple and downright handsome as that, should just simply go to waste.

If people in general agreed with him, none came forward to say so, and while it was a certainty that other men admired her physically, there was nothing under the sun that disenchanted and disillusioned men as much and as swiftly as a masculine woman. Elisabeth L gave orders like a man, thought and acted and even re-acted as incisively and as pragmatically as a successful businessman, and those were things men simply did not appreciate in a woman. Maybe they feared the competition or were unsure of their ability to compete with her. Or maybe it was simply that men just did not like the idea of an assertive female, but whatever it was they managed to avoid Elisabeth L by the hundreds and it evidently did not displease her one bit.

Sixty square miles of good rangeland, the quality cattle to stock that kind of an empire, her interests in Buffalo and elsewhere, plus all the other things she had to keep her occupied from morning until night, would have been enough to squeeze aside additional entanglements of any kind, for anyone.

CHAPTER 2

A Matter of Doubt

The Cumberland Transportation Company had been founded by Douglas McLeod, and eleven years later he had lost it in a poker game to a man name Framingham, who had in turn sold it to an eastern combine.

It had been successful from the beginning and still was despite the ominous sounds of the encroaching railroads. The steam cars, it was said, would never put the stage lines out of business simply because the railroads would never put spur-lines to all the little two-bit towns and settlements. Coaches would be plying their routes back and forth between outlying communities, and railroad depots, forever.

Maybe. The reason Cumberland Transportation Company was especially successful in the locality around Buffalo was because old Lodestone McLeod had planned it so that it could cover the best distances by the shortest of all possible means, which meant it could cross his ranch, and the competing lines hadn't been able to, so in the end the competing companies had simply gone out of business.

Years afterwards when several range fires had allegedly been started by careless smokers pitching cigars or pipe dottle or even cigarette butts out of the coach windows, when the McLeod interests no longer were concerned about the Cumberland Transportation Company, there grew up an increasing degree of antagonism between the company and the owners of the Ludston land holdings.

Several legal attempts to force CTC to re-route its coaches over to the public north-south roadway had failed in courts of law. After each of those expensive lawsuits SM range had caught fire in the late summer when all Big Valley was tinder-dry.

The last time there was one of those racing, deadly conflagrations Elisabeth L had hired a range detective by the name of Horn to ascertain, if he could, whether the fire had been deliberate or accidental.

It had been deliberate, Horn had reported six weeks later, and the man who had paid the incendiarist was a major stockholder in CTC named Forrest Bishop.

Typically, Elisabeth L bought passage on a CTC coach, rode to Butte where the company had its headquarters and without warning at all strode into the private office of Forrest Bishop, told him who she was, told him that if there was ever another fire on her range she would personally see to it that he was horse-whipped within an inch of his life, since that was apparently the only kind of logic he understood, then she had gone back to the way-station, got aboard the next outward-bound coach and had returned to Buffalo without incident.

Only two people knew of this incident for a very long while. For three years in fact, then in the late dry autumn of a near-drought year there was a fire on the extreme northwesterly part of SM range, and it had been burning for three days before word reached the ranch. By then it was out of control and the best Elisabeth L could do was hire townsmen by the wagonload, send them up there with her riders, provide cooks and grub, fire-fighting implements and good wages in a desperate battle to save her autumn feed.

She lost the battle.

'Fifteen sections burnt out,' the rangeboss reported when the last wagonload of townsmen had been paid off and hauled back over to Buffalo. 'Fifteen square miles, Ma'am, of fall feed down to ash. And it started right alongside the gawddamned right-of-way the way they all start. I talked to six different folks who was passing through on the coaches and saw how it was burning at first, right up alongside the right-of-way on both sides. Set afire as sure as I'm a foot tall.'

Elisabeth L said, 'Why? Give me one reason, Art. We haven't had a bit of trouble with CTC in several years.'

'We *always* got trouble with CTC!' he exclaimed. 'Ever since I can remember, and before that as well. They have been forcing a fight with SM since your granddaddy's day and it's common knowledge they want to get their right-of-way declared a public easement.'

That was true enough, but it was a general confrontation, and right now, because Elisabeth L had reservations this time, she demanded more. 'Go to Buffalo,' she told him. 'Take a couple of men with you, and talk to the way-station manager down there. I want to know which coaches passed through for the full week of the time when the fire started. I want to know the names of the drivers and the gunguards on each of those coaches.'

Art Campbell rode out of the yard with a pair of seasoned men and Elisabeth L watched him depart, her mood less bleak than usual because she still did not believe that this time, it had been a deliberate fire. *Why* she felt that way she could not have logically explained. Nor would she have tried to do so.

The list of whips or guards would give her something to deliver to a hired detective. It would then be up to him to determine whether or not any of those men either knew he'd hauled an incendiarist across her range, or had himself had any hand in setting her land afire, or had halted his stage so that someone else could get out and set her land afire.

Of course if the arsonist were experienced neither the driver nor gunguard would even suspect they'd hauled him in their coach, and they would not have had to halt to allow him to start the fires; he would simply have pitched ignited firebrands or something like that out of the coach windows at intervals.

Other passengers would have seen him;

no matter how skilled he might have been he could not light firebrands and toss them out without the other passengers being interested.

The trick then was to determine whether or not a solitary passenger had ridden a Cumberland stagecoach across SM range on the way down to Buffalo. Elisabeth L correctly surmised the coach had been heading *for* Buffalo, not away from it, from the way the fire had burned and from the direction it had clearly started from.

She was busy with her thoughts, her deductions, and the paperwork which inevitably followed in the wake of her desperate and futile effort to save her autumn feed, during the absence of Art Campbell and the men who had ridden into town with him.

She did not forget having sent him to Buffalo, but when suppertime arrived and the *cosinero* rang his bell and she heard several men whoop loudly and laugh in the yard out front, she went to an office window to glance out.

Campbell and the pair of riders who had accompanied him to Buffalo were loping into the yard amid the shouts and amused encouragement of the other rangemen who were already on their way across to the cookshack.

If men did not arrive for meals on time, they went hungry. That wasn't Ludston law — that was an oldtime range-country law. Campbell and his companions must have heard the bell a mile or more out and had booted out their horses in order not to have to go to bed hungry.

She smiled and turned back to the desk. Men were boys grown tall.

Later, she went to her own kitchen and prepared her own meal. Her father and grandfather had eaten with the men. If she had been a man, she probably would also have eaten with them. She wasn't a man. No one could ever possibly make the mistake of thinking she was one, either.

Campbell came around to the office door after full nightfall was down and she admitted him, turned up the lamp, offered him a chair near the front of her big old desk, and re-seated herself in strong silence, clasping both hands atop the desk eyeing the rangeboss.

'Wouldn't give me the list,' Art said, and smiled at her as he leaned, fished in a pocket and pulled out a torn and crumpled piece of paper. 'There it is.'

She ignored the paper he placed on top

of the desk in front of her. 'How did you get it?'

'Not like you're thinking,' he replied, still smiling. 'There is a hostler in the corralyard down there I used to ride with twelve-fourteen years ago. He got hurt in the back and had to take jobs on the ground. I gave him two dollars for the list and he made it up himself off the company logs while he was having a beer across the road. Then he brought it over.'

Elisabeth L nodded, leaned to open a drawer and delve inside a tin box for a pair of silver cartwheels. She handed them to Campbell and he was correctly reimbursed. Then she closed the desk-drawer and picked up the list. As she scanned it she said, 'Have you read this?'

He had. 'Yes'm.'

'And did you see any names that you thought might be worth hiring a range detective to investigate?'

'No'm. I didn't see a name there that means anything to me. But those are just the coachmen. Seems to me they'd be unlikely to start a fire, but it also seems to me it'd be a little hard for them to haul some feller around who *did* set fires, without them boys knowing it.'

She glanced over the top of the paper.

'What are people saying in town?'

Art Campbell shifted position in the chair and crossed one long leg over the other one. It never troubled him at all to tell her something he knew she would not like to hear.

'They are saying SM is getting its just desserts.'

She sighed. 'Thank you for bringing back the list, Art.' She showed him to the door, and after he had departed she went back to the desk to study those names again, but they meant as little to her as they had meant to her foreman, and the longer she thought about it the less she felt inclined to pour good money after bad; she was almost convinced, without any reason actually, that it had not been arson.

But there was another consideration. She had made a threat and a promise, unless she kept them . . . but only two people knew she had threatened Forrest Bishop, she and the CTC executive, and if his conscience was clear about the fire he would not be expecting trouble with her.

She rose and went to a window to gaze down across the starbright big empty yard. There was a bright light over at the log bunkhouse, and at the cookshack the *cosinero* was either cleaning up after supper or perhaps he was setting sourdough to rise.

The world as far as she could see was peaceful. It was old and serene, hushed and peaceful, which was how she liked it to be.

She blew down the mantle of the office lamp and headed for her bedroom. She had made no definite decision about the fire. Perhaps she would awaken with a ready-made solution in mind. It happened occasionally.

People would expect her to take some kind of action. Art Campbell and her riders would expect it. The people over in Buffalo would expect it.

There were times and this was certainly one of them when the enigma of being something beyond a woman, above and beyond being a woman, demanded something of her which she did not feel like giving and which in fact she was not going to give.

Her prestige might suffer, it probably would suffer. Over in Buffalo and upon the roundabout ranges she could imagine people saying she had lost her nerve or she had been frustrated, had been out-smarted by the stage company. They would then go on to predict that within a short length of time Elisabeth L would lose her power and her strength, would be fair prey.

Her mother had told her several times that a human being cannot be successful and also be weak. Well she wasn't weak. She had not changed one iota — she simply had no proof, and did not believe any proof existed, that the fire which had destroyed two-thirds of her autumn feed had been deliberately set.

And those who thought otherwise and who sought to make some kind of an issue of it by intimating that Elisabeth L was softening finally, was turning vacillating and indecisive — weak — were going to get a surprise the first time they decided to encroach a little — and they would, she felt sure of that because the neighbouring cowmen had been testing her every year or two ever since she had come into full ownership of the Ludston holdings and the Ludston grass.

She went to bed looking bleak and feeling the same way. The first of the small lines around her eyes and at the outer limits of her handsome full mouth, were deepening a little at a time bringing on an expression of indomitable, unyielding, uncompromising toughness. The kind successful cow*men* showed.

CHAPTER 3

A Beating

People waited. They had reason to know that when Ludston grass was destroyed or Ludston land had been violated or trespassed upon there would arrive a swift and certain retaliation.

This time more than ever they knew it would happen; that had been the autumn feed for those thousands of head of SM cattle. Burning the feed, this time, had been a cripplingly successful tactic, more successful than ever before.

They caught Art Campbell and the other SM riders either in town or upon the range and showed their almost masochistic concern. All the men from SM could say was time would tell what Elisabeth L's reaction would be, then Campbell and one other SM rider, Sam Harrelson, encountered a stranger named Bishop riding out over the burnt sections upon a big brown horse with the CTC neck-brand, and when they approached the stranger from different directions, guns drawn, and ordered him to dismount first, then give an account of his presence on SM land, they were setting in motion a series of events which would touch not just the lives of Campbell and Harrelson but the lives of a great many other people including Elisabeth L.

The man on the CTC horse was somewhere between Art Campbell's age and Sam Harrelson's age. Sam was an SM tophand, tough and capable, perhaps about forty, and one of Art's trusted tophands. The man standing at the head of the CTC horse wearing drover's low-heeled boots, a tie and brown coat, unarmed as nearly as his captors could see, looked about thirty-five or thirty-six. He was heavy in the shoulders, thick in the arms and legs, and had curly dark hair and slate-grey eyes. When he was asked his name all he said was, 'Bishop,' and this did not at the time mean anything to either of the armed rangemen throwing down on him.

'What are you doing out here?' Campbell demanded to know. 'Where did you get that horse?'

The burly man looked around. 'The horse? I borrowed him from the way-station manager over in Buffalo. He's a stage company animal.'

'Yeah, I can see that,' stated Campbell. 'Mister, lift your coat.'

Bishop obeyed. 'I'm not armed if that's what you want to know,' he said, proving it literally then allowing his coat to drop down again. 'What am I doing out here? Well, I'm trying to determine what caused this fire.' Bishop gestured on all sides of where they were standing. 'It must have burnt out of control for many days. It's nothing but ash as far as a person can see.'

Art holstered his sixgun, pushed with both hands atop the saddlehorn and gazed steadily at the dismounted man. Finally he said, 'Are you a stage-company man?'

The stranger inclined his head when he replied. 'I work for Cumberland, yes, but the way you make it sound, I'd have to be an employee of the devil and that's not correct at all.' Bishop's gaze never once left Art Campbell as he spoke on. 'I can see the SM brands on your horses so I can guess where you're from — the Ludston ranch — and I'm aware of the bad feeling between CTC and your cow outfit, but CTC had absolutely nothing to do with starting this fire. I'm here to try and determine who did start it, or at least how it got started.' Bishop turned slightly to look at Sam Harrelson, who was still holding an aimed sixgun. 'I'll tell you again, CTC did not have a hand in it.'

Art Campbell softly, almost indifferently, said, 'You're a gawddamn liar,' then he swung to the ground from his saddle. 'Fires don't much start by themselves.'

The stage-company man reached in a pocket and drew forth a discoloured, thick broken piece of heavy amber glass. 'You're wrong, my friend, they *can* start by themselves. You see this thick piece of glass? It looks to me as though it probably came from the base of someone's broken and discarded coal-oil lantern. A thing like this lying in the grass beside the trail, if it got tilted just right, could catch sunlight, particularly this time of year when the sun's very bright and hot, and through a process of magnification start a fire which wouldn't look like much at first . . .'

Bishop stopped speaking. The pair of rangemen were staring stonily at him without seeming to be listening. When he went silent, gazing from one rangeman to the other, Sam Harrelson said, 'Did you just say we was liars, Mister?'

31

Bishop showed some frank surprise. 'Liars? No, of course not.'

Art offered a contradiction. 'Yes you did. A minute ago when I said fires don't much start by themselves, you said I was wrong.' Art casually took a forward step. 'That's calling me a liar, Mister.'

The stage-company man gazed a moment almost with regret upon the piece of half-melted glass in his hand, then he slowly pocketed it and raised his slaty eyes to Art Campbell's tough, weathered and bronzed countenance. 'I'm not here for trouble,' he quietly said. 'That's exactly what I'm here to try and prevent. CTC did not start this fire.'

'You're a lyin' bastard,' said Sam Harrelson from the saddle, and leaned as though to dismount as he also holstered his Colt.

When Sam swung off Art Campbell used this slight diversion to move ahead. He was within a yard or so of the CTC-man when Sam Harrelson ambled up and said, 'Hey, Mister.' When Bishop turned, Art swung.

The blow caught the stage-company's man along the back of the neck and staggered him. He stumbled forward almost colliding with Sam Harrelson, who looped a vicious punch into Bishop's middle, then, as Bishop doubled forward to protect his soft parts, Harrelson drew his sixgun and lazily swung it overhead, but this time he missed because Bishop seemed to have anticipated something like this; he was drawing away sidewards when the pistol-barrel blurred past the right side of Bishop's head.

Sam looked chagrined and turned to chase Bishop. Art Campbell blocked the injured man's additional withdrawal. When the gasping, injured CTC man tried to get clear, Art fired a blasting right fist from shoulder-height. It made a solid, meaty sound when it connected. Bishop stopped retreating and sprung his thick legs wide to remain upright. He was badly hurt and although he tried his best to turn one way or the other to avoid the additional beating he was too hazy in the head successfully to do it.

Sam, who had never once acted in haste, did not move swiftly now as he stalked the glassy-eyed man with his uncocked Colt partially upraised to swing it overhand in a clubbing motion.

In a disdaining tone Art Campbell said, 'Hold it, Sam, I want to have some fun with the grass-burnin' son of a bitch.'

Harrelson obediently stopped and let his

gun-hand drop away.

Art came forward standing erect, both fists at his side. When he was five feet distant and closing, the CTC man made his first offensive attempt, he seemed to grit his teeth as he suddenly rather clumsily side-stepped, then turned back just as Art was coming after him also sidestepping. Art walked head-on into a big, hard fist. It caught him completely by surprise. He and Sam had been positive they had beaten the battered stage-company man beyond any show of resistance.

The blow made Campbell's air blast outward, it brought him forward and downward with both arms protectively across his stomach.

Sam finally moved swiftly, and this time when he swung his sixgun he was hurrying to strike before the CTC man could finish off Art Campbell.

Bishop tried to get away but Harrelson clubbed and clubbed again, swinging his sixgun as though it were a battle-axe.

Bishop could not escape. One blow numbed his right arm from the shoulder down, another blow brought a spurt of blood from alongside Bishop's head, and the last time Harrelson swung although the

CTC man did everything he possibly could do, the gun-barrel ground down across the top of his skull.

Bishop dropped, caught himself on all fours and dazedly tried to lift his head, to look for his adversary so that he might be able to avoid the next strike.

He was too far gone. Blood dripped from two places where Harrelson's gun-barrel had torn the flesh and when his eyes refused to focus he did not see Sam step across and aim the last overhand strike. That time, blood flew from the injured man's torn scalp and Bishop pitched forward on to his face as though he were a gut-shot bear.

Sam turned. 'Art, you able to ride?' he asked, and stepped up where the rangeboss was slowly straightening up. 'You all right, Art, can you ride?'

Campbell nodded.

Harrelson went after their horses and as he passed the big brown CTC horse he kicked hard, catching the unsuspecting brown horse in the stomach. The horse flinched, then turned and fled, reins flying, stirrups flopping.

Art Campbell took the reins of his animal and leaned a moment upon the horse's left side as he said, 'Ought to kill him, Sam. We'd ought to shoot him where he's lyin'.'

Harrelson looked around and down. 'He's got a hell of a long walk ahead of him to reach town, and in his shape I wouldn't bet no money he'd ever make it. I think we done enough.' Harrelson turned back. 'You need a hand getting on?'

Instead of replying the rangeboss turned a stirrup, toed in, grabbed the horn with one hand, the mane with the other hand, and hoisted himself over leather. He looked pale enough to be sick to his stomach. Apparently the CTC man could hit hard.

'That'll teach the son of a bitch one thing,' Art stated, reining around. 'Not to step a foot on to SM land, and not for any stage-company louse to come anywhere near you and me again, after what they did up here.'

The sun was slanting away on its downward trajectory as they reined back southward in the direction of SM's home place. Sam Harrelson rolled a smoke and lighted it. 'You see that thick chunk of glass he had?' Sam asked the rangeboss. 'Now that I think about it, something like that *could* start a fire. I never thought about that before. A thick chunk of glass lying in the dry grass — when the sun come around to where it would shine through that glass . . . when we was kids that's how we used to start our cook-out fires, Art.'

Campbell looked disdainfully at his companion. 'Now tell me you don't think that son of a bitch didn't bring that piece of glass along with him and figure to use it to clear CTC?' Campbell gently shook his head. 'Sam, there wasn't any other thick glass lyin' around out there. I never saw any, did you? Well, CTC sure as hell was successful at burnin' us out beyond what they figured to do, so they had to turn aside any blame. Folks would be up in arms if they knew CTC deliberately did that.'

Harrelson inhaled, exhaled, decided to tell the truth and said, 'Not any folks I know, Art. Around Buffalo and even on the range folks don't give a copper-coloured damn how SM and CTC end their feud.'

Campbell did not yield. 'All right; maybe SM isn't the most popular cow outfit in Big Valley — but the facts remain the same. And CTC won't look so good in other places if it gets out how they tried to ruin a cow outfit over here in the Big Valley country.'

Harrelson gave up arguing. He didn't care to argue about an issue he did not feel should have been handled any differently. 'All I'm saying is that SM and CTC will probably have to battle this down to the wire by themselves. No one's going to buy in when they don't have to. It'll be up to us, Art.'

Campbell, who was beginning to feel better, finally, smiled mirthlessly. 'That would suit me just fine. Me and Miz' Bedford. If everyone else will stay out, we'll run that Cumberland Transportation Company plumb out of business.'

Harrelson was interested. 'How? They own a right-of-way or whatever it's called — an easement — to run their coaches across SM. That's common knowledge, Art. How can you put them out of business when they got it all their way?'

Campbell's answer suggested that being hit so hard in the stomach may have augmented his hatred of CTC. 'By gawd we'll dig a trench across their easement every fifteen feet, Sam. They'll be forever just getting one stage through!'

Harrelson blew smoke, looked admiringly at the rangeboss, then smiled broadly.

CHAPTER 4

The Return to Buffalo

Summertime was the most lavish epoch of all Montana's seasons and all the interludes between the seasons such as that windy, blustery period between spring and summer.

'Winter-Count' which was the oral tradition of a man's life among the Indian tribesmen, was often commemorated upon a deer or antelope hide, and each fierce winter the man lived through was particularly noted because Montana, like adjacent Canada, was noted for hard winters.

Summertime had the ability to banish all the bitter memories. It was greener and more fecund and more thoroughly enchanting than summertime anywhere else. A summertime in Montana was like a beautiful woman — something a man remembered for the remainder of his life exactly as he saw it just that one time;

perfect, unchanging, completely magnificent without flaws.

Montana was not as large as Texas nor as varied in its landscape as California, but it *seemed* every bit as large — and different. It had a turquoise sky most of the time which was hugely rounded and immaculately without blemish. The vistas were crystal-clear for hundreds of miles. It may have been as an old man said, a period of such shortness that Montana's summertime had to exceed in bounty and beauty and spirituality summertime anywhere else.

It was kind to people. In direct contrast to the terrible winters when a man on foot, sore and sick and beaten could not have walked three or four miles without collapsing to be discovered when the snow melted off in springtime, the same injured individual could walk and rest and walk again, always find cold water to drink at creek-side, always find a shady, fragrant place to lie and rest, and finally be back-tracked by the marks left by that fleeing saddlehorse.

It might take the better part of a day before the backtrackers were successful, but it could be done without much effort, and meanwhile Montana's bland, warm day

40

and the fragrant, sweet air did a lot towards alleviating the man's discomfort.

He was, in fact, freshly washed and made presentable beside a little snow-water creek when they rode up leading the CTC horse, and sat their saddles eyeing him. He did not look any worse than most men who got bucked off horses, which was what they had decided had happened to him when the CTC horse had returned in riderless disarray to Buffalo.

The leader of the rescue trio spat amber, considered Bishop a long while in total silence, then gestured for the man leading the riderless horse to hand down the reins.

His name was Abraham Alford, he was massive, bearded, tough and knowledgeable. He was the Cumberland Transportation Company's way-station manager down in Buffalo. Being better than six feet tall and more than two hundred pounds in heft, and fearless, made Abe Alford a formidable individual. He was mightily respected on the range and over in town. Also, he was one of those people who had never had a doubting moment in his life; he had always been confident, self-assured, and capable. Now, eyeing the husky man on the ground, he finally said, 'Mister Bishop, your paw never was

41

much of a horseman either.'

That was all Abe Alford had to say about what he felt certain had been an accident resulting from poor horsemanship. On the slow ride back he would gaze at the younger man and shake his head.

The pair of corralyard-hostlers with them were youths, sinewy and reticent and alert. Whatever their thoughts they kept them to themselves which was always a pretty good idea in the company of a man like Abe Alford.

Bishop figured out what they thought had happened to him and was quite content for them to believe that fallacy. It eliminated the need for a lot of explaining.

On the other hand, as they rode along he asked Abe Alford a number of questions about SM, its riding rangemen, its owner, and its reputation.

As far as Abe Alford was concerned, CTC should have broken the back of the Ludstons years back when it might have been possible to do that. Now, as he said, regardless of whether the Ludston holdings were administered by a female or not, there was too much wealth and influence and power.

'Stir them up now and they'd import a small army of gunmen and not even CTC could match them at something like that.'

'CTC has been sniping at them, though,' said Bishop. 'Range fires, inconveniences, court rights over the easement.'

Abe denied none of this, but he was a stoutly loyal company man, so he said, 'It goes back more years than I am old, but the Company didn't start it. All we ever done was protect ourselves and — well — maybe strike back a little.'

'Like fifteen square miles of burnt-off autumn feed?' said Bishop.

Abe glowered. 'Mister, you don't sound much like a Company man. No, to my knowledge CTC didn't have no hand in what happened back there to her autumn grass.'

'Would you know if CTC had been responsible?' asked the burly, younger man, and again he got that glowering dark look.

'The kind of questions you're asking,' he said, 'you'd better get the answer from your paw. I didn't much favour his notion of sending you over here in the first place. We've handled trouble with SM before.'

'But not fifteen sections of it, Abe, and not the kind of trouble sure as hell could arise over all her fall feed being burned off,' stated Bishop. 'If she decided the Company did it this time, I think she

43

darned well might import that small army you were talking about. I think most big cowmen would react like that.'

Abe shrugged. 'She's a woman, not a man. But if she brings them in — what can anyone prove against CTC?'

'Since when do hired gunmen need any kind of proof?' asked the younger man. 'Since when do they even *care* about proof, Abe? Hired gunmen take pay to kill people and who the victim is or why he is supposed to die don't have very much to do with anything.'

Alford rode along flintily watching Buffalo's rooftops firming up in the shimmery distance. The afternoon was well advanced but the heat seemed to increase rather than decrease as the day waned. He had no more to say until they were nearer to Buffalo's outskirts, then he asked a question.

'You'll be heading back now, Mister Bishop?'

The burly man answered slowly and evasively. 'It's beautiful hereabouts this time of year, Abe. I've always liked the Big Valley countryside in summer. Seems a shame to hurry away just when full summertime is everywhere.'

Alford turned. 'You don't happen also to collect butterflies?' he asked sourly, and before an answer could be offered a man's cry high up the northward roadway drew attention to the visible appearance of a rusty red CTC stagecoach careering southward towards town in a high lope.

Abe watched a moment, spat amber and cursed a little. 'Damned fourflushers we got driving the coaches nowadays. Look at that; there's no more reason for him to dynamite those horses like he's doing than there is for me to fly to the moon, except that it looks good to the folks down in town and all the schoolboys'll follow a coach-driver around like he was Buffalo Bill Cody or something as colourful and all.'

Bishop watched, and gently smiled. Alford was undoubtedly correct, but it looked colourful indeed, and even romantic, to see an honoured old scarred stagecoach like that one go rocketing down through the Montana sun-brilliance in the late afternoon with mountains behind it and a green overhead sky above where the thin tawny dust arose.

Abe turned to the pair of young corralyard-men. 'Go on ahead,' he ordered. 'Lend a hand when the coach gets to the yard.' He then walked his horse along beside his companion watching the younger riders head out in a swift lope.

He continued to watch the coach and the pair of men he had dispatched to assist the other corralyard-men as he said, 'Mister Bishop, do us all a favour and just head on back to Butte and tell your paw SM's got nothing to tie that darned fire to us with. And leave sleepin' dogs lie.'

'Suppose Miss Bedford looks at it differently, Abe?' said the younger man. 'The idea in me coming down here in the first place was to make certain CTC was not responsible, and after I'd determined that, also to make certain Miss Bedford was convinced of it so that she wouldn't arbitrarily decide to shoot our horses or burn our corralyard in Buffalo, or maybe cut up our easement so that stages couldn't use it — or do any of the dozens of other things which could hinder the hell out of us.'

Abe Alford shifted his cud of chewing tobacco and continued to peer far ahead from squinted eyes as he spoke again.

'I don't feel she's going to do anything. But even if I was wrong, even if she decided CTC was responsible and then she made up her mind to retaliate — do you think for one minute you riding out there would move her off centre one little bit?

No Sir, it wouldn't. You'd no more influence Elisabeth L than I'd fly to the moon. Either way, Mister Bishop, she's got her mind made up by now. If it's that CTC isn't responsible, then there won't be no trouble. If it's that we *are* responsible, take my word for it not a blessed thing you could ever say to Elisabeth L would change her mind at all.'

Abe spat aside, glanced at his companion, then shrugged massive, thick and powerful shoulders. 'All right, you're goin' out there. Well, I owe your paw something so I'll ride along with you. And I'll tell you right now, if there is trouble, you and me are going to get shellacked within an inch of our lives. She's got a foreman and five damned tough rangemen out there. The two of us won't stand the chance of a snowball in hell.'

Bishop smiled, ran a set of bent fingers through his thick head of hair, adjusted his torn and soiled coat, turned his horse down Main Street beside the way-station boss and rode into the corralyard beside Alford where he swung off and handed his reins to a hostler.

Abe said, 'Mister Bishop — this here isn't no liverybarn. You rigged out that horse, you'll un-rig it and take care of it

47

yourself.' Abe turned on the hostler. 'You got plenty of things to do which don't include lookin' after anyone's saddle animal. Get on about your work.'

Evening was approaching, there was a noticeable scent of cooking in the air, now, and in the middle distance to the west of the corralyard and beyond its mighty pole fence out back, a woman's tired-sounding voice called to a lad named Jack to get into the house and wash up before his paw got home.

Bishop cared for the CTC saddlehorse, then crossed out of the corralyard in the general direction of the little hole-in-the-wall cafe south of the harness works where he had been getting his meals since arriving in Buffalo, and ate lightly. Ordinarily he was a strong eater. This evening his stomach was a little queasy so he favoured it, and afterwards when he walked out front to smoke in the settling late dusk and look up and around, Buffalo was beginning to change from a daytime town to a nighttime town.

The roadway was relatively empty and quiet; a few light rigs and a horseman or two were still out there but this time of day when most people were at home for supper, even the plankwalks were pretty well abandoned.

That stage which had arrived with a flourish over at the corralyard was still being re-fitted with a fresh hitch, and its passengers were either standing out front upon the opposite sidewalk looking Buffalo over, or they were hurrying to a bar or a cafe to fortify themselves for the resumed journey when the coach would be led forth into the roadway again.

The burly man in front of the cafe made a cigarette and enjoyed it, then he strolled towards the rooming-house where he had a change of attire in his room, and a chance to get a bath out back in the log house.

He ached and he was tired, and his mind was as clear and purposeful as a two-edged dagger. He was by nature a thoughtful and quiet man. He was also by nature a bad man to take advantage of.

While he was out back in the old log house immersed in bathwater, thinking and planning, several SM riders arrived in town for a few drinks and perhaps a few hands of faro, poker or twenty-one. He did not know they had arrived and he did not see them because after bathing he went to bed. He was tired and sore and it had been a wearisome as well as a harrowing day.

Elsewhere, Abe Alford saw the SM riders appear over in front of the saloon, but Abe paid them no particular attention. He had his desk-work to do before he could also go over there and have a nightcap. By the time he got to the bar the SM rangemen had departed, and even if they hadn't it still would have meant very little to Abe.

CHAPTER 5

A Ride to SM

Leo Bishop had been in Buffalo three days before anyone saw him wearing a shellbelt and holstered Colt beneath his coat. As Abe Alford said to one of his corralyard hostlers as he twisted to watch Bishop coming across the road from the direction of the rooming-house, 'Well, in one way at least he's commencing to act human. Now if he'd just quit wearin' those frock coats he'd keep from lookin' like the darned undertaker . . . Muley, go saddle us up a couple of saddle animals and when they're rigged out let me know at the office.'

Abe then strode over to intercept Leo Bishop and herd him into the office which fronted upon the roadway diagonally opposite from the saddle and harness works. There, Abe had a pot of coffee on the wood-stove, and with nothing more than a grunted greeting until he had filled two cups and passed one to the younger man, Abe sceptically eyed his first visitor of the morning.

'You must have fallen pretty hard when that darned horse jumped you off,' he observed. 'You got a black-and-blue swellin' on the side of your head.'

Bishop tasted the coffee. He happened to be on hand the day Abe made a fresh potful. The coffee was tasty so Leo ignored the remark about his discoloured upper cheek and commented upon the coffee. Abe was not susceptible to flattery and never had been.

'When it's poisonous as often as it seems to be when I make it,' he stated, 'there has got to be a time or two, accordin' to the law of averages, when it ain't.' Abe glanced out the rear-wall doorway and saw the yardman shuffling forward. 'Mister Bishop,' he said, 'are you still set on riding out to SM?'

Leo finished the coffee. 'Right now, this morning,' he replied. 'If you're too busy here in town . . .'

Abe put down the coffee cup. 'Come along,' he said, and led the way out where the hostler had left the pair of saddled and bridled CTC animals. As he untied one of them and passed over the reins he said, 'Mister Bishop, if there's trouble out there today, mind my word, you're going to get that elegant coat dirtied-up and maybe torn.'

They left town by way of a westerly road and had a deep, broad expanse of unchanged rangeland on three sides as they booted their beasts over into a little comfortable lope in order to get across as much of that territory as they reasonably could before too much of the morning was spent.

SM's headquarters had been screened from visibility in the direction of Buffalo by the deliberate action of Elisabeth L's grandfather. He had not wanted to have to look at a settlement, he had said, from his porch, and for that reason he had placed the sprawling log buildings beyond a low, long landswell and had then planted trees, mostly unkempt tamaracks, on the far side of the landswell to further inhibit the view in the direction of town.

It was not actually much of a ride from Buffalo to SM headquarters. When they slackened pace Abe Alford pointed to the long ridge of scraggly trees and announced that SM's headquarters was just beyond and through that windbreak. Then Abe recited the legend of old McLeod's dislike of settlements being responsible for the ranch buildings to be out of sight, down the yonder slide of that slope where the tamaracks were.

Leo Bishop had said practically nothing on the ride out, except a couple of times when they encountered small bands of SM cattle and horses. He had commented upon the obvious quality of the critters, to which Alford said, 'Folks can complain about the Ludstons all they like, but when it comes right down to basic facts, they've done a darned sight more for this territory than anyone else I ever heard of. They was the first to breed up the quality of beef, and they brought in the first registered studhorses and bred up the size and quality of the horses . . . it's just that they also been sort of stand-offish — and I even figure that's their right, too.'

Leo looked at his massive, bearded and rather formidable companion. 'You're defending them, and yesterday on the ride back you were —'

'No,' broke in the corralyard boss in a growly tone of voice. 'No, by gawd I'm not defending nobody. I'm simply givin' the devil his dues. I'm simply statin' the facts, and if a man ever gets to the place where he can't be honest at least with himself, he's in a hell of a condition. The Ludstons have done a lot of good. Anyone who claims otherwise either hasn't been in Big Valley long or else they aren't being honest.'

They were coming down through the tamaracks as Abe made this final comment. Ahead of them and slightly downhill out across the vastness of the ongoing rangeland were the SM ranch buildings, big and massive, scattered and grey-weathered to blend with the autumn landscape, and except that this was summertime, they could almost have seemed to have been some kind of natural phenomenon.

Bishop said nothing but he looked and made obvious assessments, and as they came across a broad trail leading directly to the yard, he gave his first judgement.

'Whoever founded this place had a feel for the land and his place on it.'

Abe Alford looked a little surprised, spat aside and offered no comment.

Two large dogs came to the edge of the yard and barked. A balding man came forth from the cookshack profanely to order the dogs back. They obeyed him, went up on to the cookshack porch near him and dutifully sat down to watch Abe and Leo enter the yard and ride up in the direction of the long, low main-house. When they were passing along in front of the cookshack the cook called over to say, 'No one's around, so if you got something to say you'll have to settle for me, or not say it at all.'

Abe looked, then sighed and reined towards the balding man. 'They must have left awful early,' he opined.

The cook was an unsmiling individual. 'No they never leave early,' he stated. 'This here is a working ranch, Mister, and no one sets around much after sunup.'

Abe said, 'That's not early?'

The cook scowled. 'I told you, Mister, this here is a working cow ranch. No, sunup ain't early.'

Leo Bishop broke in. 'What is the foreman's name?'

'Art Campbell,' replied the cook, shifting his mildly hostile eyes. 'He won't be back likely until near to evening. This time of year they got plenty of work to do out across the range.'

Leo described the two men who had beaten him. 'Is one of those men Art Campbell?'

The cook nodded. 'Yes Sir. And the other feller's Sam Harrelson, our tophand.

Him and Art ride out together a lot. Why, Mister, you want to see either of them fellers?'

Leo smiled. 'I'd like to see both of them.'

The cook raised a scrawny arm. 'If it's important, Mister, you can head southwest. You see those dark brush-patches out yonder four, five miles from here? Well, down the far side of the marking ground. I heard Sam say him and Art would be out there this morning getting things ready. We'll be bringing in the cattle over the next couple weeks for marking and altering.' The cook dropped his arm and stared at Abe Alford. 'Aren't you the feller who bosses CTC's corralyard in town, Mister?'

The suspicion in the cook's voice was clear to both the horsemen sitting just beyond the porch. Abe smiled coldly through his dark beard as he said, 'You got in mind maybe shooting me in the back when I ride out of here if I am?'

The cook reddened. 'If I was to shoot you, Mister, it sure as hell wouldn't be in the back. And if you're a CTC man, you're not in a very healthy place right now — not after our autumn feed just got all burnt off.'

Abe glared. 'Who said CTC had anything to do with that?'

Before the cook could reply Leo Bishop put another question to him. 'Where is Miss Bedford?'

The cook looked from Abe to Leo, then said, 'She rode out right early this morning and I don't have no idea where she went.' He turned again towards Abe Alford. 'No one has to say CTC had a hand in burning off that grass, Mister; CTC is the only outfit around who'd do a thing like that.'

Abe bristled but Leo was reining away westerly when he said, 'We're right obliged to you,' and slid his glance to Alford. 'Come along, we've got a few more miles to go.'

They left the yard under the cook's disagreeable stare. Abe whittled off a fresh cud and cheeked it, then folded his wicked-bladed clasp knife to return the thing to his pocket as he said, 'That wasn't no welcoming committee back there.'

Leo shrugged. 'You knew it wouldn't be.'

Abe eyed the younger man, rode along for a while in thoughtful silence, then stroked his beard as he seemed to arrive at a conclusion before he finally spoke again.

'Mister Bishop — you wasn't bucked off that horse yesterday, was you?'

Leo looked up shaking his head. 'No.'

'All right. And it was Art and Sam gave

you those bruises and lumps, wasn't it?'

Leo thinly smiled. 'You'd make a good Pinkerton detective, Abe.'

'And now,' stated the big massive bearded man, 'we're on our way to look up those two and settle scores. Isn't that about it?'

'Yes,' conceded Leo. 'But you don't have to feel obligated. It was your idea to come along, not my idea.'

'Alone out here, this time they'd have killed you,' stated Abe Alford.

Leo offered no rebuttal. In fact, he said nothing at all. He kicked out his horse and led the way at a lope all out across the sunbright grassland until they were heading up a low rise where a number of brush patches flourished, then he hauled back down to a walk.

Abe was grim. He did not glance at his companion again. His entire attention was upon all the vast open rangeland around them. He seemed to expect to find more SM riders beyond the brush-patch knoll, but when they topped out up there all he could make out in the middle distance was a pair of riders near a scrubbed-off piece of ground perhaps ten acres in size where a small creek ran, and where someone had stacked about a cord of firewood for branding fires.

There was a boulder-ring out there with black earth and black char within it to mark the spot where SM branding irons had been getting heated for more than a generation or two.

'Looks like a traditional marking ground,' said Leo, and Abe Alford answered without taking his eyes off that pair of distant horsemen.

'It is. I expect there's been more thousands of calves worked on this stretch of ground than anywhere else in all Montana Territory . . . that is Campbell, the feller on the chestnut, and the man turning in the saddle to watch us now, that is Sam Harrelson . . . if you have in mind taking them on, you've picked the toughest pair on SM. It's a good thing I'm along.'

Leo loosened his reins so the CTC horse could lower its head and slog along at a decent walk. He watched the other horseman down there also turn and look back where he and Abe were descending the far side of the brush-patch slope. That one, he knew even at this distance was Art Campbell. He studied both men and finally said, 'Abe, I'm glad you're along too. But not for the same reason you have in mind. I want Harrelson on the ground and I want him unarmed and without any interruptions.

But I don't want you to light into Campbell. All you have to do is make certain Campbell stays out of it until I'm ready for him.'

Abe looked pained. 'What the hell are you talking about?' he grumbled. 'You're making it sound like you got no doubt about whipping the tail off Sam Harrelson. Well, let me tell you something . . .'

'Keep it to yourself,' ordered Leo, gauging the narrowing distance. 'Abe, just throw down on Campbell and keep him in his saddle. That's all. We'll disarm them, then I'll take them down off their horses one at a time. You understand?'

Alford spat, dragged a limp sleeve across his chin and put a wondering, slightly doubtful, slightly puzzled look upon the man he was riding with. 'It's your headache,' he finally grunted. 'All right, I understand. And if they clean your plough, don't expect me to help out unless they pile on to you two at a time.'

When Abe finished speaking the two sets of horsemen were less than a hundred yards distant from one another. Elsewhere, there was not a soul in sight.

CHAPTER 6

An Interruption

Leo Bishop's frock coat, which lent him an appearance of dignity and made him look a little as though he might be a minister or, as Abe Alford had noted, like an undertaker, also had another use. Leo palmed his sixgun as he and Abe rode up where Campbell and Harrelson were waiting, kept the gun partially concealed by the coat until he halted the CTC horse a few yards away from the baffled-looking SM riders, then he raised his right hand and they saw the gun as it emerged from the folds of the coat.

Leo said, 'Pitch down your handguns, Gents.'

Neither of the SM men moved. They were both staring steadily at the man in the frock coat. They had reason to remember him.

Leo cocked the sixgun. 'Throw them

down,' he repeated, more softly this time, more distinctly ominously.

Harrelson looked at the rangeboss and Art Campbell eased back in the saddle to obey, to lift out his sixgun and let it fall. Sam Harrelson did the same. Leo smiled at them. He gestured towards the tophand. 'Get down. Hand your reins to Campbell.'

Harrelson obeyed again, still without saying a word. Neither of the SM men had offered to speak up to this point. They did not offer to speak now either, but they exchanged a look as Sam handed up his reins, and as Harrelson peeled off his riding gloves as though he knew exactly what was coming and faced forward towards Leo Bishop.

Abe Alford was scowling. He was probably doing it unconsciously. When Leo looked over, Abe reluctantly lifted out his sixgun and carelessly pointed it towards SM's rangeboss. When he said, 'Stay in your saddle,' he sounded more disgusted with himself than with the rangeboss. Abe Alford was one of those big men who always felt a little as though he were cheating when he resorted to guns instead of his ham-like fists.

Finally, Art Campbell broke his silence.

'By gawd, you *are* a CTC man,' he said to Leo Bishop.

'I told you I worked for Cumberland,' replied the burly man as he handed his reins up to Abe Alford and systematically removed his frock coat, folded it and laid it across his saddleseat, then methodically removed his shellbelt and holstered Colt. 'I told you that yesterday, Mister Campbell.'

Leo Bishop smiled and moved forward towards Sam Harrelson. He was not quite as tall as the tophand but he was heavier by at least thirty pounds, and he was compactly powerful, light on his feet, and, today, neither of the SM men had dazed him by any unexpected strikes.

Sam Harrelson moved a little, shuffling left then right, fists upraised, eyes narrowed. He was clearly no novice at this sort of brawling. When he thought he had his prey in range he lightly sprang ahead and swung a looping strike.

Leo Bishop got under it, and as Harrelson recoiled Bishop moved with surprising swiftness for a thick and heavy man. He fired a blow into Harrelson's unprotected right side over the ribs. The strike came from more than two feet away but the sound it made was of a powerful blow being aimed at a drum, and SM's tophand wilted, then back-pedalled as quickly as he could.

The three onlookers, including the recipient of that powerful blow, had just made a discovery. Leo Bishop could hit as hard as a mule could kick, and he could do it from a distance no greater than a foot or two from his target.

Harrelson tried now to keep clear, tried continually to draw the thicker man off-balance and off-guard. He flicked in long-range strikes which stung but which could do no more because he would not come in closer.

Leo stalked him. After that first sledging blow it was clear to both Art Campbell and Abe Alford who the aggressor was going to be. Abe spat, chewed, and looked a little less disgusted.

Harrelson feinted to bring Leo in and the heavier man allowed himself to be baited, but he raised both thick arms to shield his head and face as he moved ahead.

Harrelson speared inward with a probing left, then grated over bone, across Leo's guard and down alongside his tucked-low head to graze that previously bruised area up alongside Bishop's head, and Art Campbell ripped out a quick, approving curse.

'You got the bastard, Sam. Tear his head off!'

Harrelson closed fast, stabbing again with the left until he had an opening, then firing the stiff-armed right fist.

He did not give ground, and this was his major error. He was beginning to believe what Campbell had yelled. He was beginning to believe he could down Leo Bishop so he stood toe-to-toe with the thicker man.

Abe spat aside, waggled his head and assumed an expression of pained disgust. Abe knew where Harrelson had made his initial mistake.

Slowly Leo Bishop came up out of his crouch beneath the taller man's lightning jabs. He went to work upon Sam Harrelson's middle with both arms, slamming in blows from no more than eighteen inches away. He drove Harrelson backwards until the rangeman's feet seemed to be unable to compensate for the unevenness of the ground. He brought the tophand's guard down and caused an expression of sick pain to appear upon the tophand's face. He did not slacken pace nor relent in his merciless attack.

Harrelson lost the ability to defend himself and instinctively backed away with both arms hanging at his sides.

There was blood at the corner of Harrelson's mouth, and in a whipped-back streak upon one cheek. Leo finally slowed his advance a little, and aimed for specific areas. He jarred the cowboy with a blow over the heart, brought blood with a fist to Harrelson's mouth, half-spun the cowboy away from him with a loose left hand, then, as Harrelson started to turn lazily back, Bishop straightened out of his crouch, stood a moment watching, then shot a blow from the shoulder. It connected with bone and skin beneath the cowboy's ear and Harrelson's legs sprung outward.

He dropped and struck hard and did not move again.

Abe Alford spat again, mopped his chin with the hand holding his sixgun, and raised a smoky look across the intervening distance.

Art Campbell had both gloved hands gripping his saddlehorn. He was staring at Sam Harrelson as though he could not believe what he had just seen happen to his tophand.

Leo Bishop strolled to the side of his CTC horse, reached into a coat-pocket over there for his handkerchief, and gently dabbed at a raw knuckle where Harrelson's belt-buckle had torn the skin. He was perspiring freely, but he seemed not to be breathing very hard at all.

No one said a word. Abe Alford with no further need for the gun in his hand, holstered the weapon and looked almost pityingly across where SM's rangeboss sat his horse like stone, gauging the burly man who was dabbing at his torn knuckle.

Campbell unwound down off the back of his horse slowly. Without saying a word he removed his shellbelt and its empty holster, then, instead of also removing his roping gloves as Harrelson had done, Campbell tugged each glove separately and flexed his hands inside each glove. He was still watching Leo Bishop in an expressionless way. It was impossible to discern whether he was fearful or whether he was confident.

Finally, he leaned, unbuckled each spur, looped them together round the horn of his saddle and clapped his hat down on top. He was making every preparation to fight.

Abe Alford seemed to have reservations. He watched everything the rangeboss did with interest and finally he gazed at his companion and said, 'If it's all right with you, I'd just as soon tangle with this one while you're catching your breath.'

Instead of replying Leo Bishop turned slightly and cocked his head in the direction of that brush-patch rib of land they had recently come down. Something out there had evidently caught his attention.

Abe also looked, and so did the waiting rangeboss with his knotted fists encased in buckskin.

There was a rider coming towards them down the near side of that landswell riding in an easy lope. Abe grunted. 'Lousy darned spectator. It'll be another SM man.' Abe lifted out his sixgun and held it out of sight behind the saddle-swells in his lap.

The rider was still a fair distance out when Art Campbell made a little surprised grunt. 'It's Elisabeth L,' he said.

By the time the other two men were willing to acknowledge that the rangeboss had said anything at all, she was well within their vision.

Abe did not return the hidden sixgun to its holster but Leo Bishop slowly took down the coat from his saddle-seat and shrugged into it despite the heat which drenched his shirtfront and despite the morning heat which had been steadily increasing over the past couple of hours.

Elisabeth drew down to a walk for the

last few hundred feet, saw Sam Harrelson flat out and face downward in the grass and concentrated on him almost to the exclusion of the others. When she finally reined to a halt and looked across where her rangeboss was standing, the question on her face was abundantly evident.

Art said, 'That's the feller who did it,' pointing at Leo Bishop.

Elisabeth L swung her glance. It was sulphorously dark and menacing but she said nothing.

Bishop explained quietly. 'Yesterday these two worked me over up where the fire burned over. Today I rode out to pay them back.' He did not flinch under her bleak look. 'If you're Miss Bedford, you'll be the one who threatened Forrest Bishop. Well, I also work for CTC and when we heard of this biggest burn-over I came out here to look — to see if I could find out what caused the fire.'

'CTC,' said Elisabeth L.

Bishop shook his head. 'No Ma'am, in the past CTC has been responsible, but not this time.'

'Who would expect you to say anything else?' she asked, then turned. 'Art, how badly injured is Harrelson?'

The rangeboss left his position beside

the saddlehorse and walked over, leaned and looked close, then shrugged. He'll make it. He's breathing and most of the bleeding has stopped. You want to help me hold him on his horse so we can get him to the ranch?'

Elisabeth L hung fire over her answer for a moment, put a long look upon Abe Alford, then leaned to dismount as though to cross over and help her rangeboss lift Harrelson.

Leo Bishop walked over, told the rangeboss to fetch Harrelson's horse up close, then stooped and hoisted the inert man and when the horse arrived Bishop eased Harrelson astride and balanced him there.

'Get astride,' he told Campbell, 'and steady him. Miss Bedford, if you'll come up on this side . . .'

She moved over and her foreman stepped back across his own saddle to rein in from the opposite side. As he turned to parallel his employer with Harrelson between them he said, 'I'll be around, CTC. The next time you come looking, I'll be around waiting.'

They walked their horses slowly back in the direction of that uphill brush-patch with Leo and Abe stoically watching their progress. Alford finally said, 'She was mad enough to chew cannonballs and spit bullets, Mister Bishop, you got one hell of a fine enemy. I don't know about your paw, but for myself I'll tell you right now, CTC is about to get a lesson in hatin' by that lady. Did you see the look on her face?'

Leo went over, snugged his cinch, mounted his horse and turned it in the direction of town without saying a word until he and Abe Alford were on the way, until it was no longer possible to see the SM people.

'That's one hell of a woman,' he said. 'I for some reason thought she'd be in her fifties, vinegary, stringy, flat in front and behind and with skin like tug-leather.'

Abe spat, chewed a moment, looked questioningly at his companion, then, whatever he'd been upon the verge of saying he did not say, and as they rode back in the direction of Buffalo the corralyard-boss acted about equal parts resigned and worried. Any man who would talk admiringly of a female like Elisabeth L at a time like this had to be plum irresponsible regardless of whether his father was a high executive with the stage company or not, and also regardless of whether he could fight better than a grizzly bear.

CHAPTER 7

A Shot in the Dark

The woman who did the laundry for the single people around town looked at Leo Bishop's shirt with the dried blood upon it and made a clucking sound of disapproval. 'If you've got to fight, you young bucks,' she said with a hint of an Irish accent, 'I'd be pleased if you was first to remove your blasted shirts. Do you have any idea, then, how hard it is to get out dried blood? Look here, it's a ruined shirt, it is.'

Leo smiled and handed the woman an additional silver half-dollar, then he departed in the direction of the cafe. It had been a full day, he hadn't eaten since morning, and the exertion had increased what was normally a healthy-enough appetite without any exercise.

Abraham Alford was already having supper when Leo appeared at the counter and stepped across the bench nearby. They nodded, then Alford went on with his eating.

A greying, hard-looking man upon the far side of Alford glanced a trifle pensively at Leo Bishop then went back to his meal. There was a lawman's star upon his shirt-front, otherwise he could have passed as an older rangerider, one of those itinerant riders who was still plying his trade a number of years after most men of his generation had either bought outfits of their own, or had got married and had moved into a settlement somewhere to blacksmith or wheelwright, or maybe bartend.

The cafeman served Bishop, and accepted him, probably because he had been serving him now for about a week and that was a long while by most cow-town standards. Otherwise, though, excepting Abe Alford, no one seemed to know Bishop nor to care whether they knew him or not. The lawman glanced over a time or two but that could simply have been the natural interest of a lawman in a stranger in the lawman's town.

Later, when Leo went out front and rolled his after supper smoke, and Abe sauntered forth to gnaw off a corner of a fresh twist of plug tobacco, the lawman

74

came up and held a match for Leo, then lighted his own cigarette and said, 'You'll be Bishop, the CTC man,' and as the lawman dropped the light and raised his eyes to meet the gaze of both the men in front of him, he said, 'I was on the west range this afternoon and ran into Elisabeth L. She told me about you cleanin' Harrelson's plough.' The lawman straightened up to his full height, nodded to a pair of men afoot who passed along behind them on the plankwalk, then fixed Leo Bishop with his hard gaze. 'My name is Ernie Pitts, Mister Bishop. I try to keep the peace in town and beyond it.' Constable Pitts made all this sound like a veiled warning. 'You tangling with Harrelson on SM's own range looks to me like CTC is out to make some more trouble.'

'Yesterday,' growled big Abe Alford, 'Sam Harrelson and Art Campbell caught this man up on the burn and ganged up when he wasn't expecting anything and beat the hell out of him, then set him afoot. Ernie, he only did what you and I would have —'

'What the hell business is it of yours?' asked the lawman gruffly.

Abe was not a man of long patience at

his best, nor did he take kindly to blunt roughness, so he reddened now when he snarled a retort to the lawman.

'Anything that's got to do with CTC is my business, and you can damned well believe that. Harrelson and Campbell went out there loaded for bear and jumped this feller without warning. Mister Bishop had a right to jump back.'

Constable Pitts inhaled smoke, exhaled it, continued to look at Abe Alford a moment longer, then turned back to Leo Bishop again. 'Now that he's had his say, Mister Bishop, I'll have mine. I try to keep the peace. I hope you aren't here to cause no more trouble between the stage company and the cattle interests, because if it looks to me like that is why you're here, I'm going either to run you off or lock you up.'

Constable Pitts started walking and when Alford would have reached to grab the lawman, Leo blocked the move and roughly pushed Abe back. He allowed Ernie Pitts to stroll well up in the direction of the saloon before he said, 'Abe, I got half what I went out there for today. If I have to, I'll settle for that. You can't always even up scores nor settle everything the way you'd like to. And there's something else: I've still got to talk

76

to the lady. That was part of why my father sent me out here.'

'After drubbing hell out of her tophand you don't stand a ghost of a chance of making her listen,' stated Abe Alford. 'I told you — Elisabeth L's about as likely to listen to something CTC has to say as I'm likely to fly to the moon.'

Leo offered no argument. All he said was, 'Does she come to town, or does she have some particular routine she follows on the range — how can I happen along and catch her away from the ranch? I don't think I'd do very good riding out there to talk to her.'

'You wouldn't for a fact,' agreed the big corralyard-boss. 'As for the other, darned if I know what she does or what her routine might be . . . hell, I think I know someone though, who would know. Beulah Lewis, the bank-manager's wife. Her and Elisabeth L been friends all their lives. Elisabeth L owns most of the bank and when she comes to town occasionally for those stockholders' meetings, Beulah usually visits a spell with her in town.'

Leo smiled and slapped the other burly man upon the shoulder. 'Find out, Abe, and I'll be around sometime tomorrow to talk to you.'

As Bishop turned away Alford said, 'Hey wait a minute. Let me advise you a little. Keep that gun on, but shed that darned undertaker's coat. It makes you look like a marryin' deacon or a plantin' one.' Abe shrugged as though slightly abashed at his own boldness. 'It's just a suggestion.'

Leo Bishop strolled the plankwalk in the direction of the rooming-house. He would have enjoyed a drink at the bar but it seemed logical that if Constable Pitts knew about his battle with Sam Harrelson others in town might also know about that escapade and he did not feel up to recounting his version of the fight. He in fact did not feel like talking about the fight at all, so he bypassed the saloon and went directly on over to the rooming-house.

Tonight a travelling pedlar out of Omaha had the chunk of lye-soap and the key to the log bath-house, so Leo had a smoke out back in the starbright bland night, sauntered to his room which was on the west side of the old barracks-like building, and had just lighted his lamp and was moving away to shed the frock coat, when someone fired at him from the west-wall window and tore half the back out of the coat, which he was holding away from his body.

He was almost pulled down when the bullet wrenched at the sturdy cloth. The sound was deafening and the astonishment made him slow about dropping and rolling to get close to the wall where that assassin out there in the night would have to lean in through the open window to get a second shot.

Someone out in the hallway squawked and ran, his booted footfalls doubly loud in the silence which followed the dwindling echoes of that solitary bushwhacking gunshot.

Leo got his Colt out, raised and cocked by the time he was close enough to the west wall to raise up a little and peer out into the darkness beyond the window.

There was no one out there. There was no second gunshot and he heard no one running over in the direction of the alleyway.

Behind him where the torn coat lay asprawl was the only physical evidence he saw until he got bold enough to get 'back upright and to move the lamp from its little marble-topped table to the top of his dresser well away from the window, then he saw where the bullet had broken a panel in the door, had penetrated it with ease and had disappeared over across the hallway somewhere.

Leo blew out the lamp, stepped through his west-wall window gun in hand and went swiftly but cautiously over in the direction of the dark alleyway. Behind him someone was knocking authoritatively upon his splintered rooming-house bedroom door and calling out in an incensed tone of voice for him to open up at once.

Around front a man in boots and who must have been rather heavy, loped up from the middle of town in the direction of the rooming-house. Otherwise, though, there was nothing; out in the alleyway there was no dust, no sighting of a man running, either on foot or mounted, not even any echoes which would indicate that the assassin had made his escape out here.

Leo stood a long while listening and looking before he turned back in the direction of the rooming-house, and nearly collided with Ernie Pitts in the darkness. Ernie peered, then said, 'Are you all right?'

Leo shoved his Colt into his waistband. 'Yeah, but it was close. He must have been standing outside the window waiting for me to enter the room and light the lamp. Why he didn't shoot when I was bending over at the lamp . . . but he didn't, he waited until I was shucking my coat, then he aimed at the coat when I wasn't still inside it.'

Ernie glanced around. 'Any ideas?' he asked.

Leo gazed a trifle ruefully at the lawman. 'All I know right now is that he had to be waiting out there, and he had to be nervous and maybe not too experienced at bushwhacking folks. Otherwise, I can't even guess.'

'I'll guess,' grumbled a bear-like silhouette advancing out of the night from the direction of the rooming-house front porch.

Constable Pitts looked, then began wagging his head. 'Not unless you saw him, Abe. Unless you saw him close enough to make a positive identification, you don't guess.'

Alford was fully clothed except for his shirt. He was a powerful man, even in his undershirt in the darkness. 'It was SM,' he snarled at the constable. 'You'd realize that if you wasn't so damned partial, Ernie.'

Leo saw the lawman suddenly whip straight up in outrage. Leo shoved forward and took a wide-legged stance between them. 'Go on back to bed,' he said to Alford, and reached to give the larger man a

81

rough shove. 'Go on, damn it.'

Abe looked surprised, then hostile, but in the end he turned away as though to obey, but he had a parting barb for the constable.

'CTC didn't have any hand in firing Elisabeth L's fall feed, Ernie, and if she gets this man killed — he's the son of one of the major shareholders in the company — and if she engineers his killing . . . !' Alford glowered, then swung and stamped away.

Ernie Pitts watched the big man's angry departure for a thoughtful moment before saying, 'Mister Bishop, if you got him for a friend around here you could do a hell of a lot worse. Now about that bush-whacking . . .'

There was nothing more Leo could add to what he had already told the lawman. 'It was deliberate, and whoever he was he wasn't very good at murdering folks, Constable. Maybe in daylight you can find some boot-tracks around here, but I doubt that, the way people are trampling all around.' Leo glanced over. 'You could do us both a favour if you would.'

'How?' asked the lawman, cocking a suspicious eye.

'You could go out first thing in the

morning and tell Elisabeth L I want to talk to her.'

'She wouldn't talk to you, Mister Bishop. Not now. I'd bet money on it.'

'She'd better talk to me, Constable, because if she don't, and if I get any suspicions that this bushwhacking son of a bitch came from SM, I'm going to do a little night-riding of my own. It's up to you — and to her.'

Leo turned, walked back to the west-wall of the rooming-house, stepped through his window and when the people who were in his room saw him like that with a gun shoved into his waistband, unsmiling and bleak, they swiftly retreated back to the hallway. He went over and slammed the broken door in their faces, shucked the sixgun and turned down the lamp, which someone had lighted after he had crawled out of the window, then picked up his trampled frock coat and irritably felt through the pockets for his tobacco and papers.

As he rolled a smoke he made up his mind that he and Elisabeth Bedford were going to talk tomorrow if he had to ride out to SM with all the hostlers from the CTC corralyard and half the available hired-hands from town to off-set SM's rangeriders.

CHAPTER 8

A Woman's Suspicions

It never took much more than a murder-attempt to make someone a celebrity in a place like Buffalo and by the time Leo Bishop got down to the cafe the following morning — in shirtsleeves because now both of his coats had been ruined — everyone along the steamy little counter knew who he was.

Abe Alford had already been in and had gone across to his corralyard, according to the cafeman, who for the first time was talkative. Town Marshal Pitts had also been in and had gone, but Ernie had been coated and spurred and ready to ride.

Leo accepted this last bit of information with interest. If Constable Pitts had decided to ride out and talk to Elisabeth Bedford he was indeed getting a good early start.

At the liverybarn when Leo walked down there after breakfast, Homer Bevans, with a lot less tact than most other folks around town, came right out and framed into words what was in his mind when he said, 'Mister Bishop, I don't recall anything like that bushwhack ever happenin' right here in town before; I'd say someone has got it in for you real bad, and from what I know about such folks and all, I'd say they'll try again.'

Leo fixed Homer with a cool stare and asked about Constable Pitts. Homer shrugged off the stare when he replied. 'He left out before I got down this morning. He's taken his horse and ridden northwest, according to my dayman. That's all I can tell you. But if you wanted to see Ernie so's to arrange for protection I'd say you was doing the right thing.'

Leo left Homer and his barn, strolling in the direction of the corralyard. If Ernie Pitts had not changed his course, he was indeed riding in the direction of SM. That was all Leo had wanted to determine down at the liverybarn. When he met Abe out back, growling because someone at another way-station up-country had neglected to grease a wheel and now he had a crystallized axle on an otherwise usable stage, Abe heard what Leo had to report with a dark scowl at the hostlers who were removing that brittle axle.

Leo said, 'Will he be able to get her to do it?' and Abe continued to glare at the sweating men beneath the jacked-up coach as he answered from the side of his mouth.

'I don't know. No one ever coaxes Elisabeth L into doing anything. She either does things because she wants to do them or she don't do them at all . . . but her and Ernie been friends a long while.' Abe heaved mighty shoulders up, then down. 'Darned if I know.' He walked over to lend a hand at removing the axle, hoisted it one-handed across the shoulder of a hostler and rigidly pointed in the direction of the corralyard forge.

'Go get Brigham and tell him we got to have this damned axle heated and re-tempered.'

Abe turned back towards Leo, strolled up with a loud sigh and cursed someone up country for all the grief Abe had encountered right after breakfast. 'I can tell, when a day commences like this one did, that before suppertime this evening I'll be up to my butt in grief. It don't fail. When you've been at this business . . .'

Abe turned slowly and gazed out

through the log gate, which was wide open, into the roadway. A pair of riders were slowly advancing from the north end of town. One of them was Constable Ernie Pitts, the other was Elisabeth L wrapped in a handsome blanket-coat of blue and white. Abe looked too dumbfounded to finish what he had started to say.

Leo guessed that Elisabeth L had probably been on her way to town when the lawman had encountered her. Otherwise, she could never have got back here to Buffalo with her companion in this short space of time.

They halted in the corralyard gateway sitting their saddles and impassively gazing over where Leo Bishop was standing. He left Abe and strolled out to them, nodded curtly and said, 'Ma'am — good morning.'

She did not take her gunmetal gaze off him as she ignored the greeting to say, 'It was not an SM man who tried to assassinate you last night, Mister Bishop.'

He offered no argument about that. 'Would you come inside?' he asked, and stepped over to offer her a hand down. She swung from the saddle with the supple grace of a lifelong rider, handed the reins to Ernie and strode ahead of Leo to the way-station office. Leo followed her inside and when she took the chair at Alford's desk he went to the opposite side of it and offered her coffee, which she refused.

He did not draw off a cupful for himself but leaned upon the wall, eyed her with candid admiration, then said, 'Miss Bedford, there is no one else who wants me dead.'

She had an immediate reply. 'I don't want that either. What would SM gain?'

He did not know. 'All right. Then it was Harrelson and it had nothing to do with SM, only with the fact that he got cleaned out yesterday.'

'Mister Bishop, he is in his bunk at the ranch with two broken ribs. He couldn't have ridden to town last night even if he had tried to make it.'

'All right, Ma'am, and how about your rangeboss? We still have a settling-up coming.'

'He was at the main-house with me, in the ranch office last evening at the time someone tried to kill you, according to Ernie Pitts.' She seemed to relax slightly as she demolished each near-accusation he made. She seemed to be forming an opinion of him which was not very flattering, too, because now she said, 'I didn't know who you were. Well, I didn't know your name until Ernie told me this morning. Yesterday at the marking-ground you didn't identify yourself except to say you worked for the stage company. Mister Bishop, I had a talk with your father a short while back.'

He knew about that talk. 'It was partly because of that talk he sent me out here when we heard someone had burned off your fall feed, Miss Bedford, and it was also partly because of my personal feeling that this feuding is ridiculous that I volunteered to come over here. Miss Bedford, CTC absolutely had nothing at all to do with burning off your autumn feed this year.'

She did not contradict him, even though he was braced for that. In fact she sat there for the first time since they'd taken over Abe Alford's office, looking at him as though he were not actually an enemy at all.

Then she said, 'Do you know a man named Donald Sanger, Mister Bishop?'

He'd never heard the name before. 'No Ma'am.'

'Are you sure?' she insisted, and he answered a little annoyedly. 'I told you — no Ma'am. What about him?'

'I think it may have been Sanger or

someone he hired who may have made that attempt upon your life last night,' she said, and looked around as Abe Alford appeared in the rear doorway as though coming in from out back in the corralyard.

Abe stopped in his tracks, blinked at them both, then without a word turned, went out into the yard and gently closed the door after himself.

Before the last of this diverting little interlude, Elisabeth L was softly speaking again to Leo even though she was not looking at him.

'I'll have to explain something to you, Mister Bishop, which won't interest you in the least. Ever since I was a child my father groomed me for the day when I would own and operate the ranch — the entire Ludston estate. He got me in the habit of riding SM range in all weather, and not just close to the buildings either, but many miles out. Sometimes I go with a rider, but most of the time I ride out alone.'

Leo agreed with her earlier premise; none of this really interested him very much, except that as she talked and as he leaned there gazing over at her, he thought she was probably the most thoroughly admirable and handsome woman he had ever seen.

'My riders are accustomed to my appearing out where they are working, Mister Bishop, and some of the time I come up on to them when they would just as soon I hadn't. Those times of course I withdraw if I can, and if I'm not seen, sometimes I can escape without embarrassment for anyone . . . Mister Bishop, Don Sanger owns the range adjacent to SM on the eastern grassland. Since the death of my parents he's been deliberately drifting his cattle over on to my grass and doing a number of other provocative things. He is testing me. I understand that; my father told me it would happen and not only with Sanger, with other adjoining cow outfits . . . I'm a woman in a man's world, working a man's ranch in a man's industry.'

Leo changed his mind about that coffee and went over to draw himself off a cup. She still refused when he offered her one.

'Mister Bishop . . . the day before my rangeboss and Sam Harrelson first met you up on the burn, I was coming across the east range in among some trees and had one of those chance encounters I just mentioned. My rangeboss and Sam Harrelson were talking with Don Sanger.

91

They didn't see me and I made sure they wouldn't by drawing back deeper into the trees and watching them.'

Leo said, 'Wait a minute. This Don Sanger has made trouble for SM before?'

She nodded. 'I told you. He runs his cattle on my grass and —'

'I mean real trouble, Miss Bedford. Would Sanger burn off your autumn feed?'

Her grey eyes lingered on Leo's face for a moment before she nodded at him. 'That is exactly what I was leading up to, Mister Bishop.'

'But why would he hire someone to take a shot at me?' asked Leo. 'He isn't feuding with CTC that I know of.'

'But SM is,' she said curtly, 'and that is common knowledge all over Big Valley.'

'So . . .'

'Mister Bishop, Sam and Art didn't have to beat you, up there at the burn the other day. I've told Art several times lately I'm not convinced CTC had anything to do with this latest burn-out. Why did he and Sam beat you, then, and why did someone last night try to shoot you?'

He smiled slightly at her. 'I'm listening.'

'It's clear enough, isn't it?' she asked,

'because if someone like Don Sanger can embroil SM and CTC in a real knock-down-shoot-out, Don Sanger who wants my land, will be the winner, not CTC and not SM.'

Leo drained the coffee cup and gently placed it aside. It had never occurred to him that there might be a third party in any of this, and right now, while he was perfectly willing to admit she was beautiful and probably clever and capable, it was still too much to have dropped on him all at once.

She sensed his scepticism because she said, 'I was coming to town this morning to look you up, Mister Bishop. Over the last twenty-four hours I think I've evolved a scheme that might help us both. I don't want to fight CTC and from what your father told me over in Butte, the stage company doesn't want a feud with me.'

He began having an inkling of what was coming. An alliance with her against someone named Sanger was agreeable, but only after he had satisfied himself through neutral sources that Sanger was indeed her enemy, and was also capable of doing what she was suggesting he probably had done — tried to embroil the stage company in a shooting fight with the Ludston interests.

'This scheme of yours,' he said to her, 'wouldn't by any chance involve me as bait, would it?'

She eyed him ruefully. 'Yes I'm afraid it would.' She was clearly expecting him to demur, so when he said, 'All right, Miss Bedford, but not for a day or two,' she seemed to be thrown slightly off balance, and to have to make some mental adjustments to her earlier assessment of him.

He smiled. 'It's terrible coffee. Are you sure you wouldn't care for some?'

She smiled. He wasn't the only person in Buffalo who had never seen Elisabeth L smile. 'I'm accustomed to bad coffee,' she said. 'Thank you.'

As he drew off two cups and took one to the desk for her, he looked her squarely in the eye and said, 'If you suspect Campbell and Harrelson of selling you out to this individual named Sanger, why don't you fire them both?'

She returned his forthright look when she replied. 'I intend to, but not until I no longer have to keep them within my sight, Mister Bishop. Isn't it wiser to keep one's enemies in sight and under control than to scatter them and run all manner of risks from them?'

He tasted the coffee, eyed her over the rim of the cup and privately decided she was not only beautiful and wealthy, she was also intelligent.

CHAPTER 9

Impressions Around Town

Because Elisabeth L was something of a local celebrity and the things which she did were of general interest around Buffalo it was probable that her discreet meeting in Alford's office at the CTC way-station with Leo Bishop would eventually be known throughout town, but when Leo crossed to the general store for some tobacco after his talk with her, only two or three people knew he had met with her.

One of them of course was Constable Pitts, and he was out front when Leo strolled forth with his fresh sack of tobacco. Ernie said, 'She was two-thirds of the way to town when I come on to her out there this morning.'

Leo nodded. He had already decided something like that must have happened. He broke the seal on the tobacco sack and went to work rolling a cigarette. 'What did she tell you on the ride to town?' he enquired.

Constable Pitts shrugged. 'Not much. She was mad about her rangeboss and her tophand overhauling you up at the burn. Otherwise, she felt SM owed you an apology.' Ernie waited until Leo had the cigarette lighted before also saying, 'I sure was surprised, her coming all the way to town just to apologize to somebody. The Ludstons were never very strong on apologizing.'

Leo got the distinct impression that Ernie Pitts was probing, was trying to draw out of Leo what he and Elisabeth L had talked about. On those grounds he said, 'Well, it wasn't just an apology, Constable. She didn't want a war with CTC and she thought there very well might be one if I got excited over that attempted bushwhack last night and sent over to Butte for hired guns.'

Ernie said, 'Ahhh,' and looked relieved. 'I figured she'd have something more on her mind. They don't waste their time, those Ludstons.' He smiled at Leo. 'Did you tell her you figured it was SM that tried to kill you?'

'I don't know who it was, Constable.

97

That's your job. I was just going to ask what you've come up with.'

'Since last night?' protested the lawman. 'I can't work miracles.'

Shortly after this little exchange Constable Pitts walked across the roadway in the direction of his jailhouse-office.

Leo had assumed Elisabeth L had left town after their talk in Alford's office. He had seen her mount the same SM horse she'd arrived in town on, and had watched her head northward up the roadway, but apparently she'd had another idea in mind because as Leo strolled up towards the corralyard now, after talking briefly to Ernie Pitts, he saw her talking to a woman up near the bank building, upon a corner where a residential intersection abutted Buffalo's main commercial roadway. She and the other woman seemed absorbed in whatever it was they were discussing. Neither of them saw Leo Bishop. Neither of them turned to look southward as he strolled up, crossed over, and stood in the shade of the stage company office's wooden overhang awning, watching. He had no idea who the other woman was. She seemed to be about Elisabeth L's age, and although she was not quite as tall as Elisabeth L she was a solidly well-built woman with a great mass of wavy auburn hair.

Eventually, they walked down past that corner heading eastward with Elisabeth L leading her saddle horse. They passed from Leo's sight and when he turned, Abe was standing there chewing and looking up in the same direction. Abe spat aside then made a pronouncement. 'That other one was Beulah Lewis, the banker's wife. Right nice woman she is. Her and Elisabeth L been friends since they was little kids.'

Abe brought his dark gaze down and around. 'I expect from now on folks will take an interest in you. When Elisabeth L rides all the way to Buffaler to talk to a man, and a stranger at that, he's bound to become sort of famous around town.'

'Or notorious,' stated Leo softly, then, in a stronger tone he said, 'What do you know about a cowman name Don Sanger?'

Abe did not hesitate at all, except to shift his cud before answering. 'Not a hell of a lot. About as much as I need to know about him. He's been frettin' with the Ludstons for years, swipin' a little of their grass now and then, runnin' his horses up into their foothill range where no one usually finds 'em until late autumn. Here in town he's a kind of troublesome feller some of the time. He hires on some pretty raunchy men each summer, and there's usually some kind of trouble.'

'These men he hires on, Abe, are they rangeriders?'

Alford squinted. 'I told you — Sanger's a cowman. Of course he hires on rangeriders. What good would a saddle-maker or a hardware pedlar be to him?'

Leo ignored the questions. It hadn't been asked because Alford expected an answer anyway. 'How often does Sanger come to town?' Leo asked, and got another of those pained, squinty-eyed looks.

'How would I know? I told you — I know as much about Don Sanger as I want to know. His kind of a man doesn't do a hell of a lot for me. I've never bought him a beer and I don't ever expect to. If I was to guess, I'd say maybe he comes to town a couple of times a week for the mail and maybe for supplies.'

Abe chewed rhythmically for a while without taking his eyes off Leo Bishop. 'How's come you to be interested in Sanger?' he asked, with a trace of frank suspicion in his voice. 'You never met him, don't know him, and as near as I can guess got nothing in common with him.'

Leo smiled. He liked Abe Alford and he

trusted him. 'Because maybe he tried to kill me last night,' Leo replied.

Abe stopped chewing. His squinted, suspicious gaze gradually widened. 'Kill you? You mean that bushwhack-attempt? What the hell are you talking about? He wouldn't know you from Adam's off ox, and you certainly haven't done anything around town to upset Sanger.'

'You said it yourself, Abe,' stated Leo. 'Sanger feuds with SM. He is Elisabeth Bedford's enemy. What better opportunity for him to promote a real shooting war between SM and CTC, than while the son of an executive of CTC is here in town, also supposedly feuding with SM?'

Abe began chewing again, but more slowly and more thoughtfully. 'Bushwhack you and SM gets the blame.' Abe stepped to the edge of the walk to expectorate, then stepped back again. 'Gawddamn,' he mumbled. 'Is that what you and Elisabeth L was talking about in my office?'

'And you can darned well keep it to yourself,' stated Leo Bishop.

Abe nodded his head. 'I never gossip,' he said. 'I like to hear it, I just don't like to repeat it. Anyway, this time it's something better left unsaid altogether.' He turned as

101

a corralyard hostler approached and said, 'That danged colicky horse is better now; you think we could risk puttin' him on the morning hitch when the coach pulls in?'

Abe looked annoyed. 'Of course not, damn it all.'

The hostler did not yield. 'We're short of a horse and I can't manufacture one. Unless we take that one, or get one from Homer to tide us over . . .'

'Go down and get one from Homer,' replied Abe. 'Tell him I'll be along directly to settle for the critter. And no darned pelter, you tell him that, too.'

As the hostler turned away Abe said, 'What do you plan to do when Don Sanger rides into town? Let me warn you a mite about him; they say he's real trouble with weapons. I know for a fact he usually has a couple of his riders with him when he rides in for supplies. You likely won't get the chance to take them on one at a time like you done out at the marking-ground.'

'Just look,' said Leo. 'I just want a look at the man, is all.'

Abe wasn't satisfied with that reply. 'What good will lookin' do you; you can't tell whether a man tried to kill you or not by just looking, can you?'

'How many ways do you know to skin a

cat?' Leo asked, and did not permit Abe the chance to reply as he stepped towards the edge of the plankwalk. 'I'll be over at the rooming-house and if Sanger rides in, send someone for me.' He kept on walking.

Abe Alford emitted a great groan, then turned with a head-wag which was reminiscent of a dog coming out of a creek, then stalked southward down towards the liverybarn. When he and Homer Bevans locked horns over the value of a borrowed livery animal being put into a CTC set of chain-harness, they needed a lot of manoeuvering ground to skirmish in.

Leo went up to the northeastward corner where he had last seen Elisabeth L and stood in awning-shade up there gazing down the east-side residential roadway to where Elisabeth L's drowsing SM saddle-horse was tied out front of a neat cottage with a white-painted picket fence. Now he knew where Beulah Lewis and her husband lived. Not that he anticipated this scrap of information ever being of any particular use to him, but he was satisfied to know where Elisabeth L's close friend resided.

He turned back, saw a battered, unkempt, huge freight wagon with twelve white mules approaching town from the north roadway, and momentarily stood to watch as the jerkline driver and his saddle-back swamper began the very slow and very accurate turning which would bring the immense old battered and laden freight wagon around to the east of town, and down the alleyway over there, with something like six inches to spare on each side.

A good teamster and his swamper could navigate that full distance without once scraping the building-backs on the west side of the alleyway or the board fences on the east side, but judging from the scars and gouges not very many good teamsters had hauled down that alleyway to the dock of the general store without leaving some scarred wood to commemorate their passage.

This time, though, the driver and his saddle-back-man up front cut their swathe just exactly wide enough. If they had missed they would have been in difficulties because they only got one chance to gauge it, and then to steer for it. Some towns had more leeway to their alley-entrances and exits, but Buffalo was not one of them.

The leaders finally stepped across their tugs in a side-pass which kept Leo Bishop standing there in awe as they set the pace and the course for the following ten harness-animals. They continued to side-pass until the swamper sang to them, then they dutifully stepped back inside their tugs and picked up the slack as the entire long caravan began to work the serpentine-hump out of its route and the leaders aimed squarely for the alleyway entrance.

They made it without touching wood and behind Leo a man's deep, pleased voice said, 'They are getting fewer and fewer, teamsters like that.'

Leo turned, did not know the man, and smiled. 'Those leaders are worth a farm in Texas,' he agreed.

The other man was about Leo's age but slighter and slimmer and was attired in city-man clothing, including a tie and button-shoes instead of boots. He offered a hand. 'Jack Lewis, of the bank,' he said. 'I know who you are — that CTC man who got shot at last night over at the rooming-house.'

They pumped hands then continued to stand and watch as that long line of leather and animals and huge old palm-wide freighter wheels slowly and inexorably ground ahead into the narrow alleyway as though the entire outfit were being fed into the town's maw a yard or two at a time.

Finally, Leo turned to walk away and Jack Lewis went back with him as far as the front entrance of the bank, and there he said, 'My paw was a freighter. I've seen him make that identical turn a hundred times, and ever since, I've come out here to watch when someone yells into the office there's a rig coming.' Lewis was handsome and somewhat boyish, especially when he smiled as he was doing now. 'Darned childish for a grown man, eh?'

Leo smiled back. 'No, I don't think it's childish. One more generation and no one will be left to handle a hitch like that any more. Nice meeting you, Mister Lewis.' He walked away thinking that if the banker's wife was as unassuming and pleasant as the banker, it was no wonder that Elisabeth L had remained Beulah Lewis's close friend after all those intervening years since they had been children together.

In fact, now that he dwelt upon it, there were very few people he had encountered around the town of Buffalo he had not liked.

It was difficult to say that about the people on the outlying cattle range, though.

CHAPTER 10

Into the Night

Leo did not see Elisabeth L leave town but when he was emerging from the cafe after supper he saw that freight outfit grinding its ponderous way southward down the stageroad and he smiled to himself over the profane concern a stage-driver would evince if he encountered one of those monumentally slow freight outfits on the roadway.

Undoubtedly the freighter and his swamper would go just as far below Buffalo as they had to in order to find good grass, clean water, and a nice supply of dry firewood for their supper fire, before they made camp. It would take a good hour and a half to strip off all that harness, neatly arrange it for morning-use, hobble or stake all those animals, then turn back to stoking up their supper-fire. It was a hard life but he had known a number of freighters and although they complained bitterly about how railroads and even transport companies like CTC had made deep, probably fatal, inroads into their hauling and cartage business, they never said they would quit.

He was still smiling to himself when he walked up in the direction of the saloon for a nightcap. Last night he couldn't have bought a drink, others would have insisted upon paying for anything he drank in exchange for his version of the bushwhack-attempt. Tonight, a dozen theories had been put forward, and another dozen assumptions as to how, exactly, that murder-attempt had been made. He entered the saloon, crossed to the bar almost unnoticed, and even the barman who served him simply bobbed his head in recognition and did not ask a single question. Such, Leo informed himself, was the perfidy of fame. He chuckled to himself and drank his nightcap, then turned dispassionately to look around the room — and met the cold, unmoving stare of SM's rangeboss across near the front-wall window at a poker table where he and two other rangemen, probably also SM riders, were idly sipping whisky and staring towards the bar.

Leo Bishop was unarmed. Even when he

was out in the countryside he did not always go armed. In town, he almost never wore his gun and bullet-belt.

The fact that a man was unarmed did not entirely preclude the possibility that he would be shot, but it made that dismal prospect much less, especially in a saloon full of men who lived according to the rule that armed men did not draw on unarmed men.

But there was another facet to this meeting in the saloon which Leo Bishop did not overlook. SM's rangeboss was glaring menacingly and with every facial indication that he was ready for battle — and there were two more rangeriders with him.

Ganging-up was not approved of either, the difference being that since Leo Bishop had no close friends in the saloon, by the time a lot of beer-drinking strangers decided they should interfere, Leo could very well be dead or half-dead, whereas the first time Art Campbell and his hostile companions drew weapons against the unarmed man at the bar, they would face at the very least a double-barrelled scattergun from behind the bar.

Leo reached, gripped his glass and downed its dregs then replaced it atop the bar and when the harassed saloonman came to ask about a re-fill, Leo shook his head and rolled a smoke instead.

Across the room one of those seated men said something curt from the corner of his mouth as all three of them kept watching the burly man at the bar. Art Campbell sneered an answer.

A moment later those three men rose casually.

Leo lit up, gauged the temper of the men across the room from him, decided that Campbell was going to risk trouble in the saloon, and trickled smoke as he drifted his glance elsewhere. There was no one in the saloon that he recognized.

He was alone.

Campbell stepped around and clear of the table. One of his riders remained back there between the table and the roadway doors, the other rider moved off casually to his right to take up a position near a little knot of unsuspecting cattlemen who were earnestly talking about something, probably the price of beef at rails-end, which seemed to hold the interest of every one of them.

Leo noted the position of the other two SM men, and waited for Campbell to approach. There was no way to tell just yet whether Campbell was going to provoke trouble with his fists or with his gun.

A large man shouldered in out of the warm night and paused to look out over the room as the little dull badge on his shirtfront reflected equally as dull lamplight.

The pair of SM men back along the front wall looked worried, and evidently Art Campbell recognized the town marshal in the back-bar mirror because he slowly turned, slightly, and headed for a different segment of the bar where he stopped between a pair of men and slowly turned to hook a boot-heel over the brass rail and with an expression of innocent indifference watch Ernie Pitts stroll to the side of Leo Bishop where they both faced the back-bar and signalled for beer.

Ernie said, 'I wasn't looking for you, but since you're here I got a little scrap of information that might interest you. Did you happen to notice a freight outfit in town today? Well, that feller and his swamper was hauling over to Bedloe couple of weeks ago and watched a couple of what they said was cowboys start a fire on the northwest sections of the grassland.'

Leo looked at the lawman. 'The SM sections?'

Pitts solemnly nodded. 'Yeah. I offered to fetch a map and let them show me on the map, but the freighter got insulted. When he needed a map, he told me, it'd be the first day he was in hell, but by the second day he'd know his way around there just as well as knows it around up here. He knew the sections and nothing I could say would budge him about those being rangemen who started that fire.'

'What in hell was he waiting for, a personal invitation to tell what he knew?' demanded Leo.

Pitts was indifferent about that. 'Don't know and don't care. What interests me is who the rangemen were — the pair of them.'

Leo lifted his eyes to the back-bar mirror and saw Elisabeth L's rangeboss glowering suspiciously as Leo and Ernie Pitts conversed. He was tempted to tell the lawman what Ernie's sudden appearance in the saloon had interrupted, but in the end all he said was, 'If they were that positive about them being rangemen, then you can bet they weren't CTC gunguards or drivers or corralyard men.'

Ernie may already have made that decision because he now said, 'Who then?'

Leo smiled. 'Who would do a thing like

that to hurt the hell out of SM? How about Don Sanger, Constable?'

Ernie sipped beer, glanced at the man beside him, sipped more beer and finally pushed the glass from him. '*She* put that bee in your bonnet this morning, didn't she?' he said, and Leo offered no denial.

'Who else, Constable? I don't know it was Sanger, and I don't know it wasn't a couple of her own men — did you see Campbell up the bar when you walked in here tonight? Go ask him.'

Leo fished out a coin and dropped it atop the bar as he nodded to the lawman and turned to leave the saloon. Midway across the room he saw that pair of SM riders fidgeting and looking helplessly in Campbell's direction as though in dire need of instructions. Leo walked right on past, shoved out beyond the spindle-doors and quickly moved to his left, down away from the front of the saloon towards the unlighted small shop southward which had a conveniently recessed doorway.

But no one emerged from the saloon.

Possibly the lawman's presence had acted as a deterrent, perhaps Art Campbell did not like the idea of walking out into the darkness where he could certainly assume someone would be waiting out there, watching for him.

Whatever the reason, the SM rangemen did not emerge, and as Leo stood in the recessed doorway waiting, he saw a pair of horsemen walk their animals down into town from the north stageroad, turn in out front of the saloon and swing down to tie up as one of them said, 'If it don't work this time we'd better just keep right on ridin' south,' and after that enigmatic comment the pair of them trooped noisily across the plankwalk and entered the saloon.

Leo finally crossed the road and went up to the rooming-house by a circuitous route. He entered the long, dingy hallway from out back near the log bath-house, went along to his room which he entered by a key, and did not light the lamp as he left the door ajar and searched for his shellbelt and Colt, then he went back out into the hallway again, locked his door and trod back the same way out of the building he had used to enter it.

In the warm night he buckled his weapon and belt into place, made all the little adjustments, then stood a moment taking the pulse of the surrounding darkness.

When he was satisfied, he made his way

back to the centre of town by a round-about route and took up a position across from the saloon. The odds were still not in his favour but they were certainly closer to being that way now than they had been earlier when he had had three stalking SM rangemen against him, armed while he was unarmed. Now, the SM riders would probably expect to meet Leo Bishop almost anywhere except directly in front of them across the roadway, when they emerged from the saloon.

But they didn't emerge, Constable Pitts did, and he proceeded to start his final round of the day upon that opposite side of the roadway, but in time he would also arrive over on Leo's side to rattle doors, and then Leo was going to have questions to answer, which he had no intention of waiting to be asked.

He watched Ernie's leisurely progress and at the same time kept his eyes upon the front of the saloon. The next pair of people to come forth into the night was that pair couple of rangemen who had arrived about the time Leo was hiding in the recessed doorway. They must only have had one drink each.

Now, as they stood in shadows and softly spoke back and forth for a moment, Leo began to have an inkling about those two. Maybe he was wrong; maybe he was beginning to see peril everywhere he looked, but the only thing he could think of right at this time, which had not succeeded was that attempt upon his life the previous night, and the remark one of those men had made, something about another failure and they might as well keep on riding, sounded very much as though they had been thinking in terms of a botched bushwhacking.

Up the opposite roadway Ernie Pitts finished rattling the locked door of the dress shop and was turning to cross over and begin his slow advance southward down the same side of the roadway as Leo Bishop was using.

A cowboy walked out of the saloon, edged around the pair of men over there talking, got his horse from the tie-rack in a very business-like manner and rode out of town by the southerly route. Everything this man did seemed to reflect a very resolute and determined mind.

Ernie was whistling a sad song called *Lorena*. He was putting all the pathos into the whistling rendition he was capable of with the result being less sad than lugubrious.

Across the road that pair of strangers stepped forth, strolled past their tethered horses at the tie-rack and struck out for the rooming-house, at least they were walking in that direction, which was all Leo needed, to break his vigil of the saloon-front and follow. He did not want to be down there anyway, when Ernie came along.

As for Art Campbell, they would meet another time.

A singing drunk staggered from the saloon bellowing the national anthem at the top of his lungs and Ernie Pitts stopped whistling *Lorena*, cursed loudly and swung off the east-side plankwalk in an unerringly ominous course for the weaving and faltering drunk. Ernie passed within yards of those two strange rangemen, and within a hundred and fifty yards of Leo and did not appear to see any of them.

When he was close enough he called to the drunk. 'Shut up that singin' you darned idiot, you'll awaken everyone in town. *I said stop that damned singing!*'

The drunk stopped in a wide-legged stance, pulled himself fully upright in a posture of injured dignity and glowered. 'Just who do you think you're talking to, my man?' he asked unsteadily.

Ernie hooked the man's free right elbow with his own left arm and jerked the drunk along with him in the direction of the jail-house. 'I'll show you who I'm talking to — my man,' he retorted angrily. 'Darn you anyway!'

CHAPTER 11

In the Night!

Leo had no trouble following those two strange rangemen and he had no trouble avoiding discovery; the strangers were too intent upon what they were about. They did not stop to look back and around even when they were up near the rooming-house.

For what those men seemed to be up to it was an excellent night. There was almost no moon — what moon there was had no more width than an oldtime scalping knife — and the lee side of the rooming-house had less starshine than almost anywhere else.

Leo dropped back as far as the alley-side woodpile and remained over there watching as the pair of strangers split up, one heading on down alongside the house, the other one hanging back where he had a good view of the roadway.

The man near the roadway was soon out of sight of his companion, and Leo decided he would stalk this one. He was confident by this time what they were up to, and he had no desire to come up behind the one alongside the house who by this time probably had a cocked gun in his fist as he stealthily approached Leo's dark bedroom window.

It was no longer possible to see that stalking man once he got midway along the dark wood wall. Visibility was inadequate for that, but where Leo was crouching he could still make out the fidgeting silhouette of the watcher, and most of the time that one's back was to Leo's woodpile as the watcher somewhat anxiously kept watch down the distant roadway where he could distinctly see the light at the jailhouse.

Leo moved out. There was some protection; an ancient and unused old wagonshed, an equally as abandoned and dilapidated old chicken-house. A pair of stalwart trees, ragged and unkempt, grew alongside the property line less than a hundred or so feet from where the stranger was uncomfortably keeping his vigil of the roadway.

Leo used each of these shelters as he stalked forward. A couple of times he had to hang fire until the watcher finished surveying the area more immediately adjacent to where he was standing, otherwise Leo had a good run at the man. He got down close enough to see that the stranger had his hand lying atop the handle of his holstered Colt, but had not drawn the thing. Leo did not follow this example, he drew his gun, moved ahead through the open territory which separated them, and when he was close enough he said softly, 'Mister — don't even draw a deep breath!' and cocked the sixgun in his fist.

The watcher turned to solid stone. He did not even lift his right hand off the Colt-handle nor turn his head.

Leo gave him a moment to recover, then ordered him to lift out the gun and drop it, which the stranger did, then he ordered the man to face the rooming-house and before the man had completed this move, Leo took a big forward step swinging his handgun. The steel barrel drove the stranger's hat down around his ears. It muffled the sickening sound of unyielding steel striking savagely against hair, scalp and bone.

The watcher fell in a heap.

Leo leathered his weapon, picked up the stranger's gun, caught the gun's owner by the scruff of the neck and dragged him roughly back the full distance to the wood-pile, leaving bootheel marks the full distance, but it was too dark for this to be very noticeable unless the watcher's friend hung around to make a concerted search, which Leo had no intention of allowing him to do.

He used the unconscious man's belt to lash his ankles with and he used the man's bandana to knot around his wrists from behind. If he'd had more time he might have improvised a gag, but the unconscious man was not going to call out for a while, and perhaps when he regained his wits, he wouldn't feel much like calling out either.

Leo hurried back down in the direction of the recent encounter with his captive. He wanted to simulate the watcher when the other one came along, but it did not work out that way at all.

The other one simply did not return.

Leo waited, watched, and finally abandoned some of his caution and slipped up alongside the building. He found no trace of the other one even though he went the full length of the boarding-house. He did, however, nearly collide with an old man tottering forth from the rear of the rooming-house walking a little rapidly in the direction of the distant privy using an old blackthorn cane to facilitate his urgent progress.

The old man did not see Leo even though they came within a yard of meeting. The old man was far too intent upon his distant destination.

Leo turned back. It did not occur to him that the other stranger might not be *out*-side, that he might be *in*side the rooming-house until he got all the way back to the woodpile where his trussed captive was feebly straining and groaning.

By then it was too late to alter his plans very much. He sat the captive up, propped him against the wood and gently laid the cold steel barrel of a sixgun against the man's cheek.

'Don't raise your voice above a whisper,' he said, 'and quit wriggling.' He held the sixgun off a little. 'This is yours; be a hell of a note being killed by your own gun.'

The bound man gingerly rolled his head around as though by doing this he might achieve some relief from the headache that blow over the head had caused.

'Who are you?' the prisoner whispered. 'I don't have much money on me.'

'Where is your partner?' Leo asked, and

pushed a little with the cold gunbarrel to expedite a truthful reply. It worked, evidently, because the man said, 'Over there somewhere.'

'No he isn't,' stated Leo. 'I just scouted up over there.'

'Then he's inside,' stated the boundman.

'To kill Bishop?'

The prisoner stopped rolling his head and turned squinted eyes. 'What's it to you, Mister, you're not the Constable.'

'I'm Bishop, that's what it is to me.'

The prisoner's eyes widened for a more intent gaze at the hat-shadowed face in front of him. He said, 'Damn it to hell,' and groaned.

'You fellers work for Sanger?' asked Leo.

'Yeah. We *did* work for Sanger, but he said if we didn't nail you this time not to come back for our money.'

Leo holstered his Colt and hunkered there in strong silence for a while. Elisabeth L had been correct right down the line. He twisted to watch the dark side of the rooming-house. The building, in fact the entire town of Buffalo, was dark and quiet now. It was closer to midnight than Leo realized.

He arose and started moving away. Now

that he knew where the other one was and why he was over there, the chance for a fair meeting was greatly increased. If he had not felt angry he might have considered going back for the constable, but these two men were not the constable's particular responsibility, not when they were so dogged in their attempt to bushwhack him.

He got to the side of the house, considered going down it to his bedroom window and forcing the confrontation there, but decided, because a window was such a limited area for manoeuvring, he would go inside the building.

He had to pass his bedroom window, though, and when he got down that far he was mightily tempted to raise up and look in.

It was dark in there, very dark in fact so it was probable that he would see no one — but he just might be silhouetted in the window-opening.

Farther along he had to bend down again to pass beneath another window, this one closed and bolted. It did not occur to him to look back as he was straightening up, and that was a mistake. At the very last moment he heard something which could have been the abrasive brush of boot-sole across hardpan earth, or which could have been a man's solid body pressing swiftly alongside the rough wooden siding. Whatever it was, he was instantaneously warned by it and palmed his gun as he was turning.

The entire night erupted into a totally black spiral of absolute silence which seemed to turn in a lazy, thick kind of spiral going constantly downward.

It was very warm. It was also very silent. For a very brief moment there was some kind of annoying rough tugging, but that passed.

Later, much later in fact, the warmth departed and an increasing chill arrived, bringing with it a grey, unpleasant variety of dismal light.

Leo rolled and opened his eyes. It was pre-dawn, also called false-dawn. Somewhere southward a rooster was raucously getting his vocal cords ready for the dawnlight crowing, and somewhere else a drowsy dog barked a couple of times.

Otherwise it was chilly and dismal and as Leo pushed up off the ground into a sitting position, he felt the throbbing pain in his head. It only occurred to him very slowly what had happened, and he chose not to think about that for a while. No man derived any solace from being caught from behind and knocked over the head by a fleeing apparition. It couldn't have been anything else. Obviously, if the man who had struck him down had known who he was, and providing the man had been that other bushwhacker, Leo Bishop would now be dead.

He had blood clotted in his hair and although he groped around he did not find his hat. His sixgun was also gone, but when he pushed upright and leaned upon the building for a moment until the whirling sensation left his mind, he saw the Colt lying off a few yards in the dust and weeds. The hat was also there.

He retrieved his gun first, checked the loads, holstered the thing and went painfully back over to the woodpile. He did not think his prisoner would still be there and he was correct about that.

For a while he considered prowling both alleyways in case his assailant and the other assassin were still in town, then, seeing that widening band of dawnlight over in the east he decided that he had been unconscious a lot longer than it had seemed, and by now his attacker and the other bushwhacker were long gone, either on southward or back to Sanger's cow outfit. He hoped it was back to the ranch.

A couple of men passed in front of the rooming-house carrying dinner-pails and quietly discussing someone's broken running gear. Leo got the impression that they worked for the local blacksmith. He waited until they were well along, then entered the rooming-house, went down the hall to his room, unlocked the door, entered, re-locked the door and went over to the wash-stand.

He shed his hat, filled the basin from the pitcher and proceeded very gingerly to wash his face and head. The gash atop his head was respectable enough, and the water started it bleeding again.

Leo packed a clean bandana under his hat over the gash, shaved, finished washing and hurled the pinkish water out the window, which was still open, left that way by the bushwhacker.

He had a headache so he could have sympathized with the man he had also given a headache to, except that his mood was not sympathetic.

A wagon rolled slowly down into town from the north roadway to presage the beginning of another day, and someone over at the saloon flung a bucket of water into the roadway to help hold down the dust later on. The water-hurler and another man, perhaps upon the opposite side of the roadway, exchanged loud pleasantries.

Leo rummaged for a pony of brandy he had put in store last week, found the bottle and took three generous swallows from it for breakfast, and also as a tonic. His head ached with an increasing ferocity, instead of doing just the opposite which he had every right to expect. The pain got worse, over the next couple of hours.

He went to bed, finally, hung a coat over the window to achieve darkness in the room, and lay back fully clothed with his Colt in his right hand upon the goose-down pillow.

Sleep was slow arriving, and if he had not been able to sleep like a log the increasing sounds of bustling Buffalo would have kept him awake. As it was he slept through a shouting match between several schoolboys, the insistent trumpeting of someone's stallion, and a dog fight which erupted not ten yards from his window.

He did not awaken until slightly past noon, and by then although the wound atop his head had swollen until it resembled a goose egg, the actual headache had almost completely departed.

He rose hungry, thirsty, and full of righteous indignation.

CHAPTER 12

Men in Waiting

Abe Alford said, 'Where you been? I sent a couple of hostlers around looking high and low for you. They even loped up to the rooming-house and banged on the door . . . Don Sanger came into town with a couple of his men and a wagon for supplies. They was around nearly all morning.'

Leo sighed. There were *dis*advantages as well as advantages to being able to sleep like the dead.

'How long ago did Sanger leave town?'

'Hour,' said Abe, and studied the younger man's face. 'You look a little drawn out. You feel all right?'

Leo ignored the question as well as the solicitous interest. 'How long would it take someone with a wagon of supplies to get back to Sanger's ranch?' he asked. 'And don't tell me it'll depend on how fast they herd the wagon.'

Abe said, 'You're in a lousy mood today. It would take about three hours to get back up there to Sanger's foothill outfit. I'd guess that about now him and his men are about half way. Why?'

'Because we're going after them,' stated Leo.

Abe's dark, arched brows climbed like a pair of broken-backed caterpillars. 'Why?'

Leo lifted his hat, lifted off the soggy bandana, and heard Alford's sharply indrawn breath, then replaced the bandana and hat. 'Because Sanger hired two bushwhacking cowboys to kill me last night, again.'

'Came closer to succeeding this time,' Abe laconically opined. 'How do you know that, anyway?'

'I caught one of them and he told me. Then I went after the other one and got knocked over the head from behind. If he hadn't been in a hurry, or if he'd taken the time to look and see who he'd knocked over the head, he'd have killed me. Sanger was supposed to pay them if they got the job done.'

Abe stroked his bearded chin and gazed at the man with the hat on as though Leo

Bishop were a variety of tribulation, some kind of a burden Abe had to live with. 'And if we catch up,' he said quietly. 'What then?'

'We'll bring Sanger back to town and I'll swear out a warrant for him.'

'Supposin' Ernie won't honour the warrant?'

'He has to honour it, that's the law. Are you going to stand around here all day?'

'No,' drawled the massive CTC supervisor. 'No, but I'll tell you right now that if we fetch Don Sanger back it'll only be after a tussle. He's got two of his men with him.'

'Pick your meanest hostler,' stated Leo, and turned. 'I'll go get a horse from out back and get saddled.'

Abe waited until Leo had gone, then ambled to his office, fished upon a high shelf for one of those little under-and-over .41 bellyguns, which he dropped into a trouser-pocket, then he took down a floppy, old black hat and put that over his shock of black hair and headed for the back of the corralyard to the bunkhouse.

A thin, mahogany-shaded man with startlingly contrasting very pale eyes was sitting upon the bunkhouse porch smoking a pipe, and watched Abe approach without moving or speaking. When the way-station boss got to the porch the bronzed man said, 'Well, now what?'

Abe glared. 'Get your damned boots on, get your gunbelt and gun, get your hat and meet me over at the corral. And don't sit there looking like I just hit you!'

Abe turned and stalked away. The thin, mahogany-shaded man rose, pocketed his warm pipe and entered the bunkhouse where he took down a booted Winchester, a belt-gun and belt, and his hat, and when the other three men in there stared with mouths agape, the dark man said, 'Abe's orders. I expect we're going out where maybe someone robbed a CTC coach. It'll be the first holdup down around Buffalo in a 'coon's age.'

The thin, leathery man walked to the corral, saw who else was rigging out over there, leaned his booted saddle-gun and went after a lead-shank and a halter. As he walked to the corral gate he said, 'Abe?' and across the poles inside the corral the yardboss said, 'What?'

'Abe, I'm not going one more damned step until you explain what this is all about.'

'Last night,' said Leo Bishop from behind the thin man and to one side at the tie-rack, 'a couple of fellers tried to bush-whack me at the rooming-house again. I asked Abe to pick his best man and to ride with me when we go talk to the feller who hired those bushwhackers . . . what's your name?'

The mahogany-shaded man said, 'Name's Clive. Clive Baggely — two "g's", but it don't pay the kind of wages a man's entitled to when he rides out with a gun on him.'

'How much more would you need, Mister Baggely?'

The thin man considered, heard the yardboss snarling inside the corral, and finally said, 'Two dollars, Mister Bishop, and I'd feel a lot better about this.'

Leo dug, produced a pair of silver cart-wheels and as he handed them to the thin man he said, 'Help yourself to a saddlehorse, Mister Baggely.'

The thin man pocketed his coins, reached to hold the gate open as Abe walked through leading an animal. Abe glared and Clive Baggely ignored that entirely to step around and also enter the corral for a horse. Abe stepped to the side of Leo and growled.

'I'll fire him, so help me!'

It did not take them long to saddle up,

but even so by the time they broke away from town and could lift their livestock over into a lope the sun was noticeably changing colour as well as location.

Abe Alford knew the countryside as well as anyone else. He led them from the roadway on an angling course so that they were facing the northeasterly far mountainsides as they loped. He also sashayed until he could show them a fresh pair of wagon-tyre marks, along with three individual sets of shod-horse signs, then he changed course again still at a lope and seemed to be taking a shortcut in the same general direction, but more eastward which meant to Leo that Sanger's ranch had to be over eastward and that Abe was aiming to effect their interception above where the unsuspecting cowman and his supply-wagon were poking along, and the ranch headquarters. There was no other way, to Leo's knowledge, for three men in a hurry to overtake, bypass, then halt and confront, three other men who were walking their horses slowly but who also had a big head-start.

He considered his course of action as they rode, decided that he probably should have sent someone out to SM to alert Elisabeth L and decided that as soon as he could spare Clive Baggely he might send him over there.

Actually, though, Elisabeth L had not mentioned having anything but suspicion about that disastrous burn on her north-westerly range, and if it came right down to it, once Leo's captive bushwhacker escaped, Leo had nothing in the way of actual proof either.

But this was not going to be a court hearing. It was simply going to be a preliminary citizen's arrest, or whatever anyone chose to call it, so that Sanger could be locked up in town until there *was* proof.

Sanger could object to high heaven. Leo had the sticky swelling under his hat to prompt him to be a lot less than amiable, and he also had the word of that bushwhacker he'd captured that Don Sanger had been behind the attempt to murder him — twice.

As far as Leo Bishop was concerned, the law could agree or disagree, he was still going to swear out a warrant and insist that Ernie Pitts lock up Don Sanger. If Ernie gave trouble, as Abe Alford seemed to believe might be the case, then Leo would himself hold Sanger over at the corralyard. And that, he knew very well, would be about as illegal as holding hostages or ab-ducting people for ransom. He had no illu-sions; if he tried this and his father heard of it over at Butte, there would be more thunder coming out of Butte than Con-stable Pitts at Buffalo could stir up in six or eight years.

They finally picked up movement several miles west and roughly parallel with them, so Abe insisted that they stretch out a little and widen the lead, which they did, and fortunately it was not as hot this afternoon as it had been previously. In fact, there was a skiff of veily clouds overhead, coming in from the north which could be the ad-vancing front of a high-country storm. They were not uncommon in Montana this time of year and it was even possible that a storm might send temperatures plum-meting and also bring a fresh covering of snow to the highest peaks.

Right now, Leo was thankful for the coolness and let it go at that.

Abe hauled back down to a walk, finally, and halted in a bosque of trees to blow his horse and also to take the time to whittle off a generous cudful of cut plug. He pouched his tobacco, offered the knife and plug to Leo, who refused, then to Clive Baggely who did not refuse, and as Clive was carving off a cud Abe lifted a mighty arm.

'They got to ford a dry-wash down yonder a few hundred yards. There's an old trail goes down in and comes up on this side.' He dropped his arm and accepted back the knife and plug, both of which he pocketed before speaking onward. 'We can stop them down in the dry-wash, or we can wait a bit until they're up out of the wash and we can stop 'em over here somewhere.' Abe spat, leaned in the saddle and gazed at Leo.

The wagon with its mounted escort was small in the distance. Leo thought it would perhaps be just about nightfall by the time the men from Sanger's cow outfit got close to the dry-wash. But he favoured halting them over there, as opposed to heading down-country, as Clive was suggesting, and ambushing them somewhere on the open range with the aid of sunlight. Clive clearly did not like the idea of going down into the dry-wash, and, in fact, most men would have viewed that as hazardous; if anything went wrong down there, there was no place for the men riding with Leo Bishop to hide before Sanger and his men could open up on them.

On the other hand, Clive had much more faith in Abe Alford than he ever would have admitted aloud, so when Abe opted for the dry-wash, and when Leo Bishop thought that was the best place to affect their ambush, Clive chewed, and studied the oncoming wagon, and rode back with the others to get down there out of sight before Sanger's crew spotted them.

It was ten degrees cooler down in the dry-wash, which might have been a welcome change if it had been that much hotter up on the range. Also, Clive saw the smooth and squiggly track of a fat snake and told the others he would bet a new saddle the snake had been one of those fat, greeny, and very poisonous timber-rattlers, and Clive kept such an intent vigil all around from then on that Leo was of the private opinion that Clive was not going to be worth much later on.

Abe went down the wash until he found a place where the crumbly bank would not cave down when he leaned to look out, and from that vantage point he finally was able to discern the oncoming riders and the wagon. They were, he told the others, about a mile and a half out and they hadn't increased their speed one iota as they came along, from the same indifferent gait they had adopted right after they had left Buffalo hours earlier.

Clive was indifferent about that. 'Why should they? What's the sense of workin' animals hard if you don't have to? Was you gents aware that this here wash is infested with timber-rattlers?'

Abe scoffed. 'What timber-rattlers? Clive, green rattlers don't come down this far out of the forest, darn it all. You saw the belly-marks of an old gopher snake or maybe an old king snake, and right away you can see a rattler behind every bush.'

Leo rose, crossed to the far bank and raised up as much as he could. Sanger's outfit was less than a mile out now. When he returned to the others he said, 'I hope to hell there will be no shooting.'

'So do I,' said Clive swiftly.

Abe glared at them both, then motioned for Clive to take their horses out of sight somewhere, take them out of harm's way just in case there *was* shooting. No one would die of thirst even if he had to walk all the way back to Buffalo, but that wasn't the point; the point was that *he* for one and presumably his companions as well, did not want to have to walk back down to Buffalo. They were rangemen, saddle-back men, and any walking at all, but particularly very much walking, was nothing any horseman ever looked forward to.

CHAPTER 13

A Difference in Men

Daylight was fast waning. It was just about as Leo had imagined that it might be; by the time Sanger and his men got close enough to the dry-wash to be clearly visible to the waiting ambushers visibility was too poor for faces to be entirely legible, even if those rangeriders hadn't all been wearing hats.

Abe Alford came back from his final look and said, 'I wish we could snag Sanger in the dark without them others knowing about it.'

Clive sniffed. 'How? You can't snaggle a leader and not have his men wonder what the hell.'

Leo had no comment. He was particularly interested in effecting this capture without gunfire. The surest way to accomplish that, he told his companions, was by total surprise. He pointed. 'Clive, get over there and flat against the wash-bank. Hold your hand on your horse's nose until it's safe not to, then throw down on them after they come down in here.'

Clive walked off leading his horse and swinging his head from left to right intently to scan the ground as he moved.

Leo sent Abe Alford over against the opposite side of the wash-bank. He did not explain to either of them that part of his strategy was based upon the very strong possibility that neither Don Sanger nor his riders would recognize Leo Bishop up close, let alone this far off in the settling dusk.

Then he drew his gun, stood close to the head of his horse and waited. When he heard them coming, heard steel horseshoes occasionally scuff against stone, heard the constant grinding sound of steel tyres moving steadily closer to the descent, he concentrated hard on being in the proper place. He hoped just as hard that Sanger's outfit would be dumbfounded.

The wagon loomed up, then its driver called softly to his team as he set the brake to skid the rear wheels and in this manner hold the wagon off the hocks of the team as the abrupt descent was undertaken.

Leo saw two riders and looked for the

third one but did not find him until the wagon was already two-thirds of the way down the dry-wash, then another rider, a thick, heavy man on a wide, solid horse loomed in the van of the rig and started down. So far, the horsemen were too intent upon keeping an eye upon the wagonload of supplies to be very concerned with much else.

There was no reason for them to be looking elsewhere in any case, since they clearly had no idea at all that they had just ridden into an ambush.

It was that thick man on the solid-built bay horse coming down in the wake of everyone else who looked casually to his left as he spoke to his companions.

'Last time I come through here there was a big old lobo wolf down here . . .'

He saw Abe Alford's forbidding bulk, menacingly dark face, and stopped speaking as he slowly reined back when Abe shoved off the crumbly wash-bank and levelled his sixgun. The thick man stopped his horse, did not take his eyes off Abe as Alford moved soundlessly over to disarm the thick man, and finally, Leo who was up ahead blocking the onward course of the others moved around his horse where they could see him, and called out.

'Evening, Gents, nice meeting you folks out here on a night like this.'

The wagon-driver set back on his lines, booted forward his wheel-brake and stared. The other two mounted men, one on each side, were just as startled, but they did not have leather in both hands and one of them, the cowboy on the wagon's off-side, very carefully and stealthily eased his right hand back.

Clive Baggely said, 'Mister, you touch that gun and I'll break each one of your lousy fingers for tryin'.'

The cowboy stiffened, then gradually looked. His companion upon the far side of the rig raised both gloved hands to the saddlehorn and kept them there in plain sight as he looked to his right, then twisted and look all the way back where Abe had already disarmed the thick man. Very gradually this rider faced forward again without looking nor acting very upset nor very surprised.

Leo tilted a gunbarrel at this man. 'Your name Sanger?' he asked.

The horseman was slow to answer but eventually he said, 'Yeah, I'm Don Sanger, and what's it to you? What is this — a robbery?'

Leo gestured. 'Get down, Mister Sanger,

and step ahead of your horse.'

The cowman obeyed. He and Leo were less than twelve feet apart. Leo gestured. 'Turn around, Mister Sanger.'

The cowman started to obey, then halted and looked suspiciously at the gun in his captor's grip. 'Just who the hell are you?' he demanded.

Instead of answering Leo stepped ahead and lifted away the cowman's Colt, then gauged his distance and swung overhand. Sanger saw it coming and tried hard to duck clear. He almost made it; he would in fact have got clear if Leo hadn't been expecting something like that and had his left arm up to block too much of a retreat.

The gunbarrel seemed to drive Don Sanger down against the ground as though it were a sledgehammer.

The man in the wagon gasped. The other two, both of them sitting their saddles under the guns of their captors, watched stonily and did not make a sound.

Leo faced the wagon. 'Pitch out your weapons,' he told the driver. 'Then get on your way.'

The driver obeyed. Farther back, that thick man looked closely at Abe Alford and said, 'Hell's fire, I know who you are, Mister. You're the way-station boss over at

Buffaler for the stage company!'

Abe showed his big white teeth in a smile. 'You must eat a lot of turnips, friend, to be able to see that well in the dark. Now shut up and set still or I'll yank you out of that saddle and stomp the waddin' out of you!'

Probably very few people ever threatened the thick rangerider and got away with it, but this time the man who was doing the threatening was a good sixty pounds thicker. The cowboy did exactly as Abe had told him to do, he sat up there and did not open his mouth again.

It was Leo who stepped aside for them to pass up out of the dry-wash. He said, 'Go on to the ranch, and don't worry much about Sanger, he'll be all right. In fact, he'll have a nice room with a bed in it tonight, and when he wakes in the morning someone'll fetch him in his breakfast. Now haul your butts out of here and don't get cute — just keep right on going until you get to the ranch. Go on, drive!'

The wagon-man clucked up his team, booted off the brake and leaned forward on the seat as though that would help. It didn't. It never did, but everyone who ever drove a wagon did it when he wanted his horses to climb an incline.

The pair of riders twisted to look back once they rose from the dry-wash upon the far side, but they made no hostile move and did not say a word. In fact, they did not speak for a long while; the men back there in the dry-wash could have heard every word spoken on a still, bland night like this one. Perhaps Sanger's rangeriders realized this and just as possibly they did not know exactly what to say until they had a mile or more in which to consider all the things which had happened back there, and meanwhile the men in the dry-wash callously got Don Sanger across his saddle, got a man on each side of him and started back.

For men who had never done anything quite like this before in their lives they carried it off very well; as well in fact as professional abductors might have done.

By the time Sanger regained consciousness they were down-country a fair distance, and although Leo had hung back, half-expecting Sanger's riders to attempt an ambush in reverse with some idea of liberating their employer, there was never any sign of those men, so Leo rejoined Clive and Abe about the time they were growling for Don Sanger to sit up and take notice and mind that he didn't relapse and fall off the darned horse because they weren't going to baby him any further.

Sanger looked over when Leo arrived. His expression mirrored suffering which was something Leo could appreciate; he too had recovered from being struck over the head with a gunbarrel.

He said, 'Coffee and whisky help a lot. We don't have any of either.' Leo turned in beside the cowman while his companions fanned out a little and dropped back, not convinced even yet that Sanger's cowboys wouldn't arrive to free their employer.

'Your mistake, Mister Sanger, was not in picking some other way to fight Miss Bedford.'

The cowman did not open his mouth but his eyes never left Leo Bishop's face. He was party to this one-sided conversation whether he acted the part or not, and as they rode, as his recovery became more nearly complete, his gaze at Leo became more unyieldingly hostile and menacing.

Leo recognized this attitude of strengthening animosity the nearer they got to town, and just before they could make out the murky outlines of square buildings dead ahead, he said, 'Sanger, what in hell do you want with more land? What good's an empire when no one ever lives long enough to benefit very much from one?'

The cowman still said nothing. If those two men could converse upon a serious topic it seemed improbable that they could ever do it amicably. The thing which would prevent Leo Bishop from ever being at ease in the presence of the cowman, was his certain knowledge that Don Sanger would not hesitate to have someone murdered who was a stranger to him, in order that he might deviously cause some kind of battle between adversaries so that when it was over he alone would be around to pick up the pieces.

Callous, indifferent murder was something Leo Bishop would never be able to rationalize about. It was inconceivable to him that anyone could deliberately plan murder. As he rode beside the cowman and occasionally glanced over at him, he got the impression that although he might have surprised Sanger, might have for the time being got the upper hand, Don Sanger was a long way from being beaten, and when they were upon the outskirts of town Sanger said something which confirmed this suspicion for Leo Bishop.

'You don't have a single charge you can lodge against me, Bishop, and if you try to get me jailed you'll regret it.'

It was Leo's turn to remain silent. Only when they were upon the north roadway did he turn and call over to Clive. 'You know where Constable Pitts lives?'

Baggely knew. 'Yeah, on the back-street. You want me to ride over and roust him out?'

Leo smiled. 'You're a fair mind reader. Bring him down to the jailhouse.'

As Clive turned off to ride away Don Sanger reiterated his earlier statement. 'You'll regret this.'

Leo shrugged. 'Maybe, but not half as much as you will the next time you send someone after me.'

Sanger threw caution to the wind when he said, 'The next time it won't be bunglers, Bishop. You'll see.'

Leo, with this candid admission still ringing in his ears, said, 'What's the point now, Sanger? You're not going to be able to use it as the excuse for CTC and SM to fight. What good am I to you now, bushwhacked?'

Sanger looked steadily at his companion as they rode down the silent, deserted dark roadway and did not say a word, but his expression showed sardonic toughness. He clearly had an answer, but just as clearly he was not going to give it.

They arrived out front of the jailhouse and swung off. Sanger turned, caught Abe Alford watching him, and snarled at the big, bearded man. 'You're a fool to let him force you into this.'

Abe answered indifferently. 'All my life I been making mistakes. What's one more going to matter?'

The jailhouse was dark, the front door was locked, and for the short while those three men stood out front awaiting the arrival of Constable Pitts there was not a sound nor a sight of movement anywhere for the full length of Buffalo's main thoroughfare.

It had not seemed this late to Leo, but then he hadn't been keeping very close track of the time, either. The fact that the saloon was dark indicated something; it was usually the last business establishment to close for the night.

There were two lights in town, down on either side of the liverybarn's wide doorless roadway opening. Those lights were very elegant having come off a fine two-horse surrey which had been wrecked in a runaway when, miraculously enough, everything else had been smashed. There were some events which were almost inexplicable, and the survival of those fine lanterns was such an event.

CHAPTER 14

Horseback in the Night

Clive arrived with the town marshal and was almost immediately shunted into the background because of the lawman's larger-than-life reaction to what Leo Bishop had engineered.

Pitts, though, was one of those fairly common individuals whose wrath was awesome for a period of roughly two or three minutes after it had first been aroused, and beyond that length of time it diminished down to a point where, by the time he arrived out front of the jailhouse, it was a steady, angry attitude without much white heat left to it. He put his hands on his hips, stared from Sanger to Alford to Bishop, entirely ignored Clive Baggely who seemed content to have things like this, then Pitts said, 'Mister Bishop, who in the hell gave you authority to go out and deliberately catch someone and fetch them along for me to lock up?'

Leo jutted his jaw in Sanger's direction. 'Ask him who hired a pair of bushwhackers to try and kill me — twice.'

Pitts didn't follow instructions; he continued to bristle towards Leo. 'Who told you that?' he demanded.

'One of the bushwhackers,' Leo replied, and walked right into the lawman's trap, because Ernie spread his arms and said, 'Produce him, Mister Bishop. Bring him in so's I can hear that story too.'

Leo wasn't stopped, he wasn't even slowed down. 'I've done better than that, Constable, I've brought you the man who hired them, himself.' Leo turned. 'Sanger?'

The cowman looked sardonically past Bishop to the lawman. 'Damnedest foolishness I ever heard, Ernie. They were out there in a dry-wash like a bunch of horse-stealing In'ians, waiting to waylay us. If we'd had any inkling believe me we'd have saved you a lot of trouble, we'd have wiped them out.'

Abe Alford glowered darkly at the constable. 'Lock him up, Ernie. Mister Bishop's goin' to swear out the warrant and you got to obey the law just like anyone else. Lock him up, or I'll fling you both into a cell.'

The constable, like most other men in town, had no desire to tangle with massive, bearded and menacing-looking big Abe Alford, under normal conditions, but this was not a normal condition. 'Don't even pretend to do that, Abe.'

Alford's attitude of menace increased to such an extent that the cowman finally said, 'I'll spend the rest of the night in your jailhouse, Ernie. Otherwise we're going to stand out here all night and argue, and I'd a darned sight rather bed down, even in a cell.'

But Pitts was not quite ready to yield even though he was now the only man out there, who was in opposition to the natural sequence of events which should follow once someone agreed to file a legal complaint. In the end, he unlocked his jailhouse, herded them all indoors, and as Clive Baggely, the last man past, walked in, Ernie glared at him.

'What the hell are you doing mixed up in this?' he demanded, and Clive weakly smiled without speaking and remained back along the front wall, a silent but interested spectator as Leo Bishop insisted upon signing a warrant for arrest, and a formal complaint charging attempted murder.

Ernie took Don Sanger into the cell-room without another word, locked him up with much angry slamming of steel doors, then he returned to hang the cell-key upon a wall-peg and say, 'Why in hell would someone like Don Sanger want to go and hire anyone bushwhacked, Mister Bishop? You got any idea who he is and how much — ?'

'If I'm dead and Elisabeth L is blamed for it on the grounds that CTC and SM are hostile to one another, Sanger comes up as a claimant at a forced sale of SM land when Elisabeth L is convicted — *if* she's convicted — but none of this would pain me very much, would it? I'd be dead and your friend in there is the one who had things planned to work out something like that.'

Ernie listened. He knew one fact was true: someone had tried to kill the CTC man. But that was all Ernie knew; the rest of it was allegation and he said so. 'I can't do a darned thing without proof. You said you talked to one of those bush-whackers — well — produce him and I'll listen, and if he convinces me, I'll start to believe. Until I get something a lot better than you've given me so far, I'm goin' to go back home to bed and in the morning I'm goin' to turn Don loose.'

Abe Alford started to comment but Constable Pitts waved him to silence as he walked to the roadside door and opened it. 'You said it before, Abe; I got to obey the law just like anyone else. By gawd, I just obeyed it.' He gestured. 'Out. All three of you. I'm going to lock the place up and go back home where decent folks are supposed to be at this hour. I did my duty, and right after breakfast in the morning I'll do it again. I'll turn Don Sanger loose. Come on — out of here so's I can lock up.'

They walked out and stood until Pitts had locked the jailhouse door. They did not say another word even when he pocketed the key, turned on his heel and walked away. Abe wanted to speak, evidently had something to say which might have been, like most of what he'd said this night, based more on emotion than upon logic, but Leo shook his head, gesturing in this way for Alford to be quiet. After the constable had departed briskly, Leo quietly said, 'We're going out to SM.' He looked hesitantly at Clive Baggely. 'You've done enough, you can head back for the corralyard if you're a mind to.'

The thin, sinewy, mahogany-coloured man commented on that dryly. 'Too late now to get much sleep before it'll be time to turn out. Might as well ride along.'

Abe simply said, 'What we goin' out there for?'

Leo led them to the horses and was freeing his animal to mount it when he said, 'Elisabeth L saw her rangeboss and Harrelson talking to Sanger. If we can't produce those damned bushwhackers we'll have to settle for second best.' He gestured. 'Clive, take Sanger's animal down to the liverybarn. We'll ride slow until you can catch up.'

They left town for the second time with the long, deep hush of late night all around and with those magnificent diamond-chip stars overhead even brighter at this late hour than they had been on their earlier exit from Buffalo. By the time Clive caught up they were a third of the way along and after Clive was with them they opened up a little and loped for another third of the way.

Abe, who had initially been unenthusiastic about this entire night-riding episode, seemed now to have reacted to being fully committed with more of his customary forthright practicability. What had made him successful as a way-station manager for Cumberland Transportation Company was now working favourably in this fresh and somewhat questionable endeavour.

They were within cannonshot of SM's headquarters when Abe said, 'Leo, there's six fellers in that SM bunkhouse, and even this late at night those are pretty big odds. Not only that, but SM don't hire mamby-pambies any more than Sanger does.'

'No sweat to that,' murmured Clive Baggely as though night-riding were second-nature to him.

Abe turned, scowling. 'Oh no?'

Clive ignored the hostile sarcasm. 'Couple of us — you and me, Abe — just step into the doorway. One turns up the lamp, the other stands in the shadows with his cocked gun . . . I slept in a lot of bunk-houses in my time and I've yet to be inside one where the fellers lay there with guns in their paws. We got 'em hands down; they got no idea what we're fixing to do. Just step in, turn up the lamp and hold guns on 'em.'

Clive made it sound as easy as it turned out to be. They didn't even rouse those two big dogs which had raised so much Cain on their former visit to the yard, and mainly this did not happen because Leo led them out and around until they came down behind the ranch's horsebarn.

Over there they left their animals at a tie-rack and only had to walk about a hundred and fifty yards to be at the bunkhouse, without a sound, and with the slightest little breeze which was blowing coming against them.

They were like wraiths, even big massive Abe Alford. Outside the bunkhouse they paused momentarily, then Clive drew his gun and stepped across the little porch, squeezed the latch until the rope-pull inside was hoisted, and Clive eased inside and whipped to one side so that Abe could move in next.

Leo, with a drawn gun, glanced in the direction of the cookshack, but there was no sign of life over there, so he shifted attention and studied the main-house. It was equally as dark and moribund-seeming. Leo then stepped ahead, shouldered around the door and flattened upon the front wall in the opposite direction from Clive Baggely.

Abe couldn't simply turn the lamp up because it had not been turned down, it had been blown out so he had to hoist the mantle, strike a match and re-light the thing. He accomplished all this without seeming to awaken anyone, but the moment the light steadily brightened a cowboy across the room northward who was lying on his side, heaved sluggishly, cursed someone for the light and rolled over.

That was all he did, though, curse and roll and go back to sleep. Clive sighed, stepped to a bunk and gently prodded a man awake with his gunbarrel. He had to prod several times. Abe crossed the room and with far less gentleness yanked a couple of men half upright by the shoulder then let them fall back. It got results; both of those startled range riders jumped their eyes wide open. Looking up into the blackly bearded, big scowling face of Abe Alford was enough to give a freshly awakened person a heart attack. It almost accomplished this now as those two rangemen stared and turned pale and did not move, did not seem to even breathe, until that man Clive had prodded awake sat up cursing and looking truculently around.

'What the hell do you think you're doing?' demanded this irate and belligerent individual.

Clive leaned and pushed the gun into the man's face, and cocked it. Clive did not smile nor look particularly hostile, but he was solemn and the gun in his fist was as steady as stone.

The man was Sam Harrelson, SM's tophand, the individual Leo Bishop had whipped to a frazzle at the marking-ground. Harrelson slowly sat up and looked around. He seemed to recognize Clive, then Abe Alford, and finally, when he leaned and could see another armed man, he made a stifled groan. He recognized that third armed man too.

They made them all sit up but there were five men not six. Leo holstered his weapon and looked closely. The missing man was the only one they had come this far to see. Leo approached Harrelson's bunk.

'Where's Campbell?' he asked.

Harrelson did not answer immediately. He seemed to be trying to surmise the purpose of those three men as he stared around the room and finally let his gaze dwell upon his questioner.

'Ain't he here?'

Leo leaned from the hips. 'One more time — then I'll split your head wide open. *Where is Art Campbell?*'

Harrelson didn't reply although he looked as though he were going to when a squeaky-toned man across the room and northward said, 'He ain't here. Ain't been here since before suppertime last night. He didn't say where he was goin' and the lady don't know because she come out to the cookshack lookin' for him while we was eating supper. And that's the blasted truth, Mister.'

Abe Alford glowered. He was an individual who did not accept frustration without showing it. But Leo was not totally defeated. He said, 'Roll out, tophand. Get dressed and don't even look like you're going to reach for that gunbelt on the wall-nail.'

Harrelson had an expression of protest across his face but he said nothing, and as he reached for his britches across the foot of the bed, Clive Baggely swung his cocked Colt.

But Harrelson did not have a hideout-gun among his jumbled clothing; he was a rangeman not a gunfighter nor a gambler, the two particular types who carried little belly-guns everywhere they went.

Leo told Abe to collect the weapons and dump them outside in the yard. He also said he would go over to the main-house, then left the bunkhouse, holstered his weapon and struck out in the direction of the main-house.

CHAPTER 15

Stuffed Cabbages!

It was two o'clock in the morning. What Baggely had said in town was even more correct now, than it had been back in Buffalo: there was not much sleep-time left in this particular night.

By the time Elisabeth L appeared at the main-house front door adequately attired she knew who was out there. She had not only demanded an identification, she had also verified it by utilizing a front-wall window.

When Leo explained, she stood in the doorway looking past him across the yard where the bunkhouse light was brightly glowing. She said, 'I have no idea where he went; he usually says something, if not to me then to one of the other men.' She swung her gaze back to Leo. 'Ernie Pitts won't hold Don after sunup, Mister

Bishop. They are old friends.'

Leo wasn't too concerned about Sanger. Not right at this juncture at any rate. He was far more intrigued about where SM's rangeboss would be; where he might have gone and why he had remained out there this long. One thing Leo was reasonably sure of — Art Campbell was not in town, and if he had gone over to Sanger's ranch . . .

'Hell,' he muttered to himself, because that could be his answer. For a fact, if her rangeboss had gone over for a secret late-night conference with the cowman of the northeasterly range, and had learned from Sanger's riders how Sanger had been ambushed and taken away by some men from town, there was a fair possibility that Art Campbell might even now be on his way to town with Sanger's riders to get Don Sanger out of jail. They would encounter little enough difficulty even if Ernie Pitts were at the jailhouse, where he most certainly would not be until after sunup. Pitts had made it plain to Leo, Clive and Abe Alford he was not going to return to his office until a decent hour of the morning.

Elisabeth L said, 'Mister Bishop — what is it?'

'I did a damn fool thing,' he told her. 'At

164

least it's possible I did a damn fool thing. If your rangeboss is part of Sanger's plot to bust you and get me killed, then he probably went over to Sanger's place tonight. If so, by now he knows CTC moved against Sanger, and what would that mean to you, if you were in Campbell's boots?'

She was slow to answer. 'Perhaps it means that my rangeboss is heading up Sanger's crew now that Don is out of it. What else could it mean, unless Art decided that with CTC and SM joining together against Sanger it might be a good time for Campbell to leave the country.'

Leo hadn't considered the escape-possibility and as he considered it now it did not appear to him as something a man of Campbell's calibre would do. That left the other obvious alternative. He decided to return to town with Sam Harrelson, lock the tophand up too, then head for Sanger's ranch and force a confrontation with Art Campbell if the SM rangeboss was up there. He did not speculate beyond the immediate aspects of what had to be done. If it turned out that Campbell was indeed no longer in the area, that would be something to face when it were proved to be true.

He said, 'Sam Harrelson will go back

with us and be locked up.'

Elisabeth L nodded, watching Leo's face. 'He and Art were close. I'm sure Harrelson was also in Sanger's confidence, at least to the extent that the time I saw the three of them meet far out on the north range, Sam was certainly part of their conversation.'

Leo smiled at the handsome woman. 'Sorry I awakened you.'

'If you'll allow me ten minutes to be ready, Mister Bishop, I'll ride back to town with you,' she said, moving as though gently to close the door.

He demurred. 'You're welcome to come along later but right now I don't want to be held up and delayed.'

She looked surprised, then annoyed with him. 'It will only take me a moment or two.'

He was turning to leave the porch when he said, 'Another time,' and hiked briskly in the direction of the bunkhouse where he called Abe and Clive to the door, told them what he thought may have happened with Art Campbell, and sent Clive to the barn to rig out a horse for Sam Harrelson. Then he looked into the bunkhouse and said, 'Boys, just go on back to sleep if you've a mind to, but whatever you do, don't grab those guns and come looking for us. You'll only ride into a lot of trouble you don't have any part in.'

He jerked his head at Sam Harrelson. 'Outside, head for the barn and don't open your lousy mouth.'

The tophand obeyed. He was fully attired, even to his hat, and riding gloves tucked into his waistband. He eyed Leo with an unhappy glance as he walked past out into the late-night empty ranch-yard, and now, finally, those two large dogs who evidently lived over at the cookshack with the ranch cook, came to life. But they were both indoors.

Clive had a horse rigged out when Harrelson came abreast of the horsebarn's front. Clive handed over the reins stonily and accepted the reins to his own animal from Abe Alford.

Leo mounted up, saw the lights over at the bunkhouse, saw another pair of lights over at the main-house as he reined around, and called to the men with him to move out.

They left the yard in a lope with a swirl of acrid dust just as the indignant and inquisitive cook came forth upon the porch of the cookshack in his bare feet, his trousers and unbuttoned shirt, with a shotgun in one hand. Across the yard a man swore with feeling from beyond the open front door of the bunkhouse, otherwise there was nothing to see but the retreating vague shadows of several horsemen, and the cook was not going to shoot at such a target even if his shotgun could have reached out that far.

He yelled across the yard. 'Hey, what'n hell happened?'

A cowboy looked out, saw starshine reflecting off twin big-bore barrels, and called back. 'We was just busted out'n bed by the gawddamn tooth fairy, Cookie.'

'Oh you smart bastard,' snapped the angry cook, and turned to curse at the dogs, then to lead them indignantly back inside to bed.

The rangeriders were dressing and arming themselves as swiftly as possible. They had to reload each weapon because Abe Alford and Clive Baggely had systematically unloaded every gun before flinging them out into the centre of the bunkhouse floor.

A grizzled, narrow-eyed man with a white scar above one eye, which seemed to pucker his eyebrow into an expression of perpetual scepticism, re-loaded first and holstered his Colt as he stepped to the side of his bunk to lean and stamp into his boots as he said, 'I been sayin' it for years — there's no darned future in this business. Even when a man's earnt a decent night's sleep, they'll rout him out every time, and for what? To get him all fired up over something someone else's gone and done. You fellers know what time it is?'

They knew. A tall younger man said, 'It's nigh to three o'clock, Carl, what the hell, we'd have had to roll out in another hour anyway.'

'All right,' conceded the scar-faced older man. 'We'd had to roll out anyway in another hour — but who pays us for rollin' out an hour earlier? No one! Who pays us for jumpin' on horses and going sashayin' all over the darned countryside in the dark maybe to get shot at? Nobody! And if one or two of us gets hurt, maybe a damned dumb horse falls on us in the darkness — who looks after us and goes right on payin' our wages and . . .'

Elisabeth L was in the doorway booted, gloved, hatted and ready to ride. She looked steadily at the scar-faced man. 'You're fired. Roll your gatherings!'

The cowboy swallowed with noticeable difficulty. Then, perhaps because he no longer had anything to lose at SM, he said, 'Ma'am, it ain't nobody's fight but your own if you'n Sanger fetch up in a range war. Men like me, we just hire on to ride and —'

'Be quiet,' said the woman in the doorway, and looked at the two remaining riders. Without Campbell, Harrelson and now that older man called Carl, she only had two rangemen left. 'The ranch is going to support CTC,' she told those other two men, one of whom was younger than she was, the other one being an older, lined and tough-looking cowboy. 'It was Sanger who burned off our fall-feed. I'm as sure of that as I'm sure that I'm standing here right now even without tangible proof. Don Sanger tried to implicate me in a bushwhacking murder as well. You can roll your gatherings too, if you wish.'

'Or,' said the tough-looking cowboy, and Elisabeth L looked steadily back as she replied to him. 'Or you can saddle up and ride into town with me.'

The tough-looking man finished reloading, slammed his Colt into leather and grinned at the uncommitted youthful cowboy. 'Just about anything beats settin' a saddle all day and snorin' all night, and just scratchin' between times. You coming along, Lee?'

The younger man rose. 'Yeah,' he said, and headed for the door.

Elisabeth L allowed them to pass out to the porch. She told them to saddle a horse for her too, then, as they departed, she and the scar-faced older man looked at one another.

She said, 'Carl . . .'

He squinted. 'You know I'm right, Ma'am.'

'I know a man is loyal to the brand he rides for,' she exclaimed firmly.

'Are you payin' me gunfightin' wages? I don't think so, Ma'am. As for loyalty — I'm loyal and you know it. But you don't own me, do you? So what right you got to make me roll out in the dark, pick up a gun and go forth like I'm something that's got to do whatever you think had ought to be done?'

She kept looking at the older man. She said, 'Are you going or aren't you?'

'I'm fired,' he replied, then shrugged. 'Yeah, I'm going.'

She didn't smile but she almost did as he grabbed a battered, old hat off a rumpled bunk and stamped past her out into the night.

At the barn, one of the other men said, 'I already saddled your horse, Carl,' and the older man stopped stone still but the cowboy turned his back slowly and led Elisabeth's animal over to her. He and she exchanged a completely impassive look. Elisabeth accepted the reins and turned to mount, which was the cue for the others also to step up across saddle-leather.

Off in the north a distant wolf-call roiled the hushed long layers of darkness coming down as far as the ranch-yard of SM as a ghostly soft echo.

A bull sent forth his high-pitched mating call and let it trail off into a series of grunts signifying that if he could not mate he would just as willingly fight, then he too dropped back into the silences.

Elisabeth L led her abbreviated riding crew in the direction of Buffalo, at a walk, and although the men following her mumbled a little to one another as they rode, she had nothing to say to any of them. Not until they caught sight of the distant paling out of a dusky sky against some black-blurred rims and saw-teeth mountaintops, then she said, 'Carl, if you're hurt riding for SM you've got a home at the ranch as long as you live.'

Carl rode and rolled a smoke, lit it and

studied the back of the handsome woman up ahead and did not open his mouth; maybe there wasn't a hell of a lot more a man had any right to expect at that, and if he maybe got killed instead of just hurt riding for some cow outfit — well — no one lived forever anyway, and what good would wages or anything else be to a dead man.

It was hard sometimes to figure out correct answers to things. Carl smoked, and refused to look at the reproachful expressions of the other two rangemen, and relented a little more as he rode along. By the time they had the murky skyline of Buffalo in sight he had just about decided his entire difficulty was the result, less of the fact that he had been very unceremoniously awakened by gunbarrels and ordered to roll out an hour early, than it was because he never should have eaten those damned stuffed cabbages Cookie had prepared as a special treat for supper last night.

Cookie was a conniving, untrustworthy, cantankerous, disagreeable, weasel-eyed bastard if there had ever been one. Him and his confounded stuffed cabbages — look what they had caused!

CHAPTER 16

The Rendezvous!

Dawn was close and although the night was at its deepest in the small hours and the pre-daylight chill was most noticeable about this time of very early morning, visibility was still limited to only a few hundred yards as Leo and his companions loped overland in the direction of the northeastward range, and because of this inability to see well, they halted every mile or so and sat perfectly quiet, trying to pick up sounds, and when they heard them, trying also to interpret them.

It was Clive in his dry way who commented the last time they halted west of the stageroad. 'When I was a kid we'd have said them was buffler. Now, I'll guess it's a band of cattle on the move.'

He was correct and as unusual as it may have been, because ordinarily cattle did not move around much in the darkness even when they could 'feel' the nearness of dawn, this time they encountered the band upon the east side of the road, and it looked to Leo to be a fair-sized herd, perhaps as many as three or four hundred head. He paused just within sight to watch.

Again it was Clive who made a comment. He evidently was the one among them who had the most experience on cattle ranges.

'That's no drift, friends, there's too many of them.'

He was right again. From the rear distance a man's fluting call rang down across the silences, and it was answered by another call far to the eastward where, evidently, someone was holding the herd to its southward course without allowing it to fan out.

Leo did not know this part of the range and said, 'Isn't it a little early in the season for a cattle drive?'

Instead of answering him Abe Alford lifted an arm. Coming towards them on the near side of the drive was a slouching rider whose attention was in the opposite direction as he hazed the near side of the drive to prevent drifting. 'Last time,' said Abe, 'he was drivin' Sanger's supply rig and we seen him down in the dry-wash.'

Leo could not make that accurate an identification from where he was sitting but he was perfectly willing to assume that Abe could. Abe, after all, had lived among all these people for a considerable number of years, if anyone were able to make this kind of an identification it should have been the way-station manager.

Then Clive stood in his stirrups, watched the drive for a moment, and eased back down saying, 'They're fixing to put this herd on the stageroad.'

The same idea evidently struck all three watchers at the same time. This was no rails-end cattle drive, this was a deliberate push of cattle in the direction of Buffalo, by riders whose employer was in the jailhouse down there. They would stampede these cattle right down through town and put everyone either back into their houses or up a tree, behind a stout fence, or to furious flight, and in the process of treeing the town some of them would liberate Don Sanger.

'Only a cowman'd think of something like this,' said Abe, watching the phantom redbacks in the middle distance. 'Leo, if we sit here much longer they'll be pointed at town like an arrow.'

Clive nodded his head. 'You can't turn 'em from behind, Gents, and if we don't move out before they get busted out in a run down the road we won't be able to turn 'em at all.'

A man's outcry came distantly, the words distinguishable as the first pearl-grey dull light brightened all along the world's uneven, distant horizon.

'Head 'em west! Hold to the road!'

Alford said, 'Damn! You recognize that voice?'

Leo hadn't, and apparently neither had Clive because no confirmation rose from either of them, so Abe said, 'Campbell! That was Art Campbell of SM!'

A rider loping through suddenly hauled back to a sliding halt. He was a long quarter mile west of the drive. He was in fact well within sight of the three motionless riders on the west side of the stageroad and saw them before they saw him. They were watching the drive, listening to the shouts, talking among themselves and had no idea they had been spied out until the cowboy suddenly whirled his horse to dash away and Clive Baggely's attention was snagged.

Clive swore, then gestured. 'Yonder's one of 'em.'

But the cowboy rowelled his horse making the animal break over into a belly-down run in the direction of the herd. Abe swore with feeling, but it had been inevitable that they would eventually be discovered since they had made no move to conceal their presence.

The cowboy called ahead in an insistent voice of warning. A couple of surprised men answered back, yelling questions. This was about the time when Leo Bishop said, 'Head for the lead and see if we can't bust this drive either easterly away from town or back north towards the foothills.'

Clive turned at once but Abe was slower in obeying; he was intently watching a horseman off on his left, northward. That rider was angling away from the drive as though he were going to have a look for himself as he headed in the direction of the stageroad.

'Hope to hell they don't have rifles,' he muttered, reining around to ride with Leo and Clive, but as the distant cowboy suddenly halted to watch those three strangers making their obvious run for the herd's head, the cowboy hauled out his sixgun and fired.

At once the herd quickened pace and many of the old mossbacks raised wicked-horned heads and rolled their eyes in near panic. A few more gunshots and no one would be able to turn the cattle, and only a fool would get in front of them to make the effort.

Clive leaned close to Leo and yelled. 'Don't wait!' Clive pulled his Colt as he said this and cocked it. 'Don't let 'em bust the damned herd down over the top of us!' Clive aimed slightly above the heads of the leading critters and deliberately squeezed two deafening gunshots.

Leo understood, then, what Clive had been saying. They had to turn back the herd, or at least force it to change course, otherwise the men behind it would soon now open up with enough gunfire far back to start the deadly stampede.

Leo looked around. Abe Alford was close, but he was watching a distant rider more intently than he was watching the herd. Leo yelled, aimed his gun at the ground in front of the leading cattle as his horse carried him along in front of them, and fired. He did as Clive had done, he fired once, cocked the weapon as he loped along, then fired again.

The cattle tried a stiff-legged halt but the pressure from behind shoved them bodily along. Leo yelled again and this time Abe Alford dug his horse and made a run bellowing at the top of his voice like a fighting bull, then he out-did both his companions by furiously charging straight at the cattle shooting his six cylinder-chambers empty.

This bizarre attack did more than anything else to terrify the cattle which were farther back. They halted, milled left and right, responded to pressure from down front by reversing themselves, and that sea of redbacks was beginning to pitch and heave, and roll, in the opposite direction just as Campbell guessed what was happening up front and began firing and shouting. The cowboys with him curved in towards the herd to do the same, but southward, Leo and Clive joined Abe Alford in charging recklessly right up into the herd, firing and yelling.

The cattle turned northward, back in the direction from which they had come. They gathered a slow, inexorable momentum. Those men farther back including SM's rangeboss had to break, finally, and flee left and right to avoid being trampled to death.

Leo had to hold the reins in his teeth as he fought to re-load while his horse continued charging against the far flank of the Sanger herd. He was successful but not without losing several bullets first. Abe and Clive seemed to manage better, but even so when three riders suddenly appeared through the shifting, undependable dawnlight to fire at them, Leo was the only one of the three who was capable of firing back. He threw up his arm, aimed as best he could, and systematically fired back as the charging horsemen swept in low behind their own murderous gunfire. Then Abe joined in, and finally Clive opened fire also. It was an even match right up until another rider appeared, then a fifth one swerved in to join the attackers, and Leo had to duck low in the saddle as that increased gunfire, inaccurate as it had to be, coming from the hurricane deck of five running horses, put more lead in the air around the three men from town than any of them had ever been involved with before.

Daylight was coming swiftly, finally. The sun would not rise for an hour or more yet, but the steely newday glow was helping visibility even though it also made judging distances a matter of considerable deception.

No one was hit in spite of the ferocity of the running saddle-back gunfight until Abe

Alford hauled back skidding his mount upon its haunches, took long aim over his forearm and fired at a gesticulating attacker engaged in urging his companions forward. Abe fired, the commanding rider leaned farther back additionally to slide his horse, then he slowly turned in the saddle, looked squarely at Abe, dropped his reins, his sixgun, and fell like a stone.

Abe was encouraged. He swung his armrest and his gunbarrel in a different direction, but he too was now a stationary target. Someone fired, stung his horse's rump, and as Abe fired the horse bogged its head and bucked wildly, flinging big Abe Alford through the air like a huge, ungainly bird. He landed on his stomach, lost his gun, his hat, and his chestful of air.

Leo did not know the extent of Abe's injury, he only saw him sail ahead and strike the ground with solid force. Leo aimed at one of those riders, fired, then called to Clive and charged.

It was a foolhardy thing to do, but during moments of agitated stress men were likely to do a lot of foolhardy things. Clive ran in behind Leo and fired to divert their enemies. Leo fired his sixgun empty and charged right through their enemies, scattering them. He chased one particular man, caught him, hauled him from the saddle and twisted so that the man was beneath Leo when they hit down. The man was knocked senseless.

Leo rose as a rider came in low, aiming his sixgun. Leo ducked, jumped ahead, caught the cowboy by the arm and hurled himself backwards with both bootheels digging in.

The cowboy came off his horse in a pinwheeling motion, but somehow he managed to land on his feet. He fought back the momentum which carried him along, tried to turn back and shoot, but Leo was still holding the man's arm and there was no way for the cowboy to get his gunhand raised enough.

The cowboy halted, dug in to whirl and aimed a vicious kick. Leo took part of that blow on the thigh, twisting to get clear of the man's boot-toe in the groin. The cowboy then hurled all his weight backwards to break free with his gunarm. Leo weighed more and effectively blocked the man, then he desperately ducked as the cowboy fired a fist and grazed Leo's head.

Finally, no longer being compelled drunkenly to stagger as they lost momentum, they both straightened up. Leo pawed the man off, wrenched away the

Colt and dropped it, then stepped ahead and ran head-on into a stiff-armed punch that jarred him to his heels. The cowboy swore and jumped ahead. Leo ducked and traded space for time until he recovered from that sledging strike.

He was waiting when the charging man struck again. This time Leo belted the man in the stomach, belted him higher, in the chest, got a handful of shirtfront and, pulled the man closer and as his head twisted, Leo struck him between the eyes. Until that exact moment he'd had no idea the man he was fighting with was SM's rangeboss. He did not recognize Art Campbell until he was bending his entire body in behind that blow between the rangeboss's eyes, and then it was too late to change anything even if he had wanted to make changes, which he certainly did not want to do.

Campbell shook like a tree in a high wind, slowly turned, glazed eyes rolling, and fell.

Distantly, the sound of that stampede sounded like thunder and even the ground underfoot reverberated. Leo had no idea what else had happened until Abe Alford limped over, stopped to speak and proceeded to re-load again as he said, 'Look yonder.' Evidently Abe was indestructible.

Leo looked. There were four strangers herding that cattle drive so that it would not change direction. Leo knew none of them at that distance.

Abe finished with the gun, slammed it into his hipholster and shed out his cut-plug to gnaw off a cud. 'Elisabeth L and three of her crew by gawd,' he announced, and pouched the tobacco into his cheek as Clive walked up his winded horse and gestured out where several hard-riding horsemen were fleeing westerly riding like the wind.

'Escapin',' said Clive in monumental disgust. 'We got a couple, and them other devils is escapin'.'

Leo smiled at Baggely. 'Let 'em go.'

CHAPTER 17

A Man, a Woman

What especially annoyed Clive Baggely was
the fact that one of those desperately fleeing
men was Sam Harrelson, the prisoner they
had brought all the way over from SM. In
the skirmish which had followed the discovery of that Sanger cattle-drive, Sam
Harrelson had escaped with the remainder
of those beaten and battered Sanger-riders.

Clive was embittered but neither of his
friends seemed to feel remorse over the
loss of Harrelson. In fact Leo went over to
haul Art Campbell upright and shove him
towards Clive as he said, 'Look after this
one, he's worth a dozen Harrelsons.' Leo
smiled as Campbell's eyes aimlessly rolled
for a moment then came down and around
to settle upon Leo. 'You backed the wrong
horse,' Leo told the rangeboss. 'You figured a man had to win against a woman

and that was a darned poor bit of judgement.'

Campbell took a wide stance and shoved clear of Clive to prove that he could stand without any assistance. 'You'll find out,' he snarled at Leo.

Abe Alford limped over. He was dirty, grey, bruised and had a black beard full of grey-tan dust. 'Campbell,' he growled, a balled-up ham-sized fist hanging ready at his side. 'Campbell, who were those two fellers Sanger hired to bushwhack Leo Bishop at the rooming-house? What were their names?'

Campbell sneered. 'How the hell would I know? What's the difference anyway? Men like that don't have names.'

Abe turned, bitterly triumphant. 'There is your answer,' he told Leo. 'The son of a bitch admitted Sanger did indeed hire those bushwhackers.'

Leo turned as riders approaching at a slow lope in a tight little bunch came down and halted where a sprawled man was lying face down. Elisabeth L pointed. 'Carl, see if he can sit a horse, and if he can help him . . . please?'

The bitter-eyed older rangerider swung off, looked at Elisabeth L and said, 'Proud to boss-lady.'

She rode on over, let her hands fall atop the saddlehorn and gazed at the rumpled, torn and battered men in front of her. She looked longest at Leo, and second longest at Art Campbell. To the latter she said, 'Why, Art? Because you still opposed a woman ruling a cow range?'

Campell turned his back and would neither answer nor look at her.

Abe Alford pierced the rangeboss's back with a menacing gaze but Leo shook his head at Abe to indicate the rangeboss was not worth the effort.

Only when Elisabeth L leaned and said, 'Art — just one question. Who started the fire on the north range?' and Art Campbell still made no move to look at her or to speak, did Leo relent a little when Alford lumbered ahead with one big hand raised. He swung the rangeboss around as though Campbell were weightless.

'Answer the lady before I tear your head off!'

Campbell's bitter glare showed unyielding hatred. 'The same two started that fire who came back to bushwhack Bishop at the rooming-house in town. You satisfied? What right you got to rule as much land as SM has? That's a man's right, not a woman's.'

Elisabeth L continued to sit relaxed, both hands clasped atop her saddlehorn. She turned slightly to give an order to her riders. 'Will you fetch up their horses so we can head for town?' as the men moved off to obey she looked at Leo. 'I'm glad you came to Buffalo,' she said simply. 'I don't suppose you know it, but Art's not the only one; neither is Don Sanger. There are a lot of men around who don't agree that a woman has any right on the cattle ranges.' She half smiled. 'Including Ernie Pitts.'

When their horses arrived there was a brief flurry of activity. One of those downed Sanger-men had a broken shoulder; riding for him had to be pure torture. Clive and Abe were willing to lend a hand with this man but neither of them offered one word of sympathy. Neither did the SM cowboys who herded along their former rangeboss and the other captives.

Elisabeth L rode in the drag beside Leo Bishop. She looked much fresher than he did, but then she'd got nearly a full night's rest and he hadn't had any. Also, she hadn't been involved in the stampede nor the fight, until both were pretty well finished.

She smiled at him. 'Mister Bishop, I

think we all owe you — and CTC.'

He looked steadily at her. 'I don't care about the others,' he said, holding her eyes with his. 'And I don't like the idea of you owing me.'

'But I do,' she persisted.

He shrugged that off. 'Who was it whose smile launched a thousand ships?'

She looked uncertain but she said, 'Helen of Troy?'

He grinned. 'How about that smile of yours launching four of five CTC stage-coaches?'

She laughed. Even Abe Alford turned in surprise. He and Clive Baggely exchanged a wise look then faced forward again.

'You have a wonderful smile,' Leo told her.

'I have a small painting of my grand-mother,' she told him, 'showing her smiling. My father used to say I looked just like her when I smiled.'

'Trouble is, Elisabeth L you don't do it often enough.'

She had an answer for that. 'I haven't had much reason to do it, Mister Bishop.'

'Could I help?' he asked, still looking steadily at her. 'All I know about the cattle business you could put on the end of a pin without any crowding. But I know beauty when I see it, and I know someone who should smile often and laugh a lot when I see them. Encourage me just a little, Elisabeth L.'

She cast a long sideways glance at him, her dark eyes glowing. 'I'm a domineering woman,' she warned.

He wasn't too concerned. 'Have you ever known a man as your equal?'

She let her gaze slide away briefly as she shook her head. 'I don't believe so.'

He said, 'Look at me!'

She obeyed.

'You know one now,' he told her.

She was perfectly willing to agree. He had demonstrated resolution, initiative, and courage. He had also demonstrated something else to her satisfaction. He was tough and durable — and he was in her eyes a very handsome man.

She murmured. 'About that encouragement . . . would you care to ride out to SM for supper tonight?'

He thought of all the sleep he had missed over the past twenty-four hours, all the meals he'd had temporarily to postpone, and all the peril he'd had to face, and decided that if they encountered no difficulties in town, and if he could make it to his quarters at the rooming-house for a few hours of sleep, and after that if he could soak in the zinc tub in the bathhouse out back for a half hour or so, he would be as good as new when he rode out to have supper with her at SM tonight.

He said, 'I'll be there.'

She smiled at him again.